# JUDE

## A NOVEL

# JEFF NESBIT

David C Cook®

*transforming lives together*

JUDE
Published by David C Cook
4050 Lee Vance View
Colorado Springs, CO 80918 U.S.A.

David C Cook Distribution Canada
55 Woodslee Avenue, Paris, Ontario, Canada N3L 3E5

David C Cook U.K., Kingsway Communications
Eastbourne, East Sussex BN23 6NT, England

The graphic circle C logo is a registered trademark of David C Cook.



The website addresses recommended throughout this book are offered as a
resource to you. These websites are not intended in any way to be or imply an
endorsement on the part of David C Cook, nor do we vouch for their content.

This story is a work of fiction. Characters and events are the product of the author's
imagination. Any resemblance to any person, living or dead, is coincidental.

ISBN 978-0-7814-1133-2
eISBN 978-1-4347-0760-4



The Team: Don Pape, Ramona Tucker, Amy Konyndyk,
Nick Lee, Tonya Osterhouse, Karen Athen
Cover Design: Nick Lee
Cover Photo: Shutterstock

Printed in the United States of America
First Edition 2013

2 3 4 5 6 7 8 9 10

092013

# Chapter One

The first time was so casual, it didn't seem real. Even now, it doesn't seem possible. But it was very real—more real than anyone will ever know.

I considered for a long time whether I could ever bring myself to talk about any of this. In the end, I came to realize that it simply didn't matter. No one would believe me.

That first time, my twin brother, Jude, and I were sitting outside on the front porch, the sun fading below the Appalachian mountain ridgeline off to the west.

I was staring at the trees that bordered our foster parents' farm. I wasn't thinking about much. Jude and I were both quiet. It had been a peaceful summer day. We were going into the fifth grade together the very next day. We'd been talking about the ghastly teacher neither of us wanted but were stuck with. "Horrible Harriet" was what last year's fifth-grade kids called her.

And then I saw it: the thing looked like a large, black crow, perched on a tree branch just over the fence line that marked halfway between the porch and the barn. But it was too big to be one of the crows that were ubiquitous in rural Loudoun County, west of Washington, DC.

Even from my vantage point, I could tell it was out of place on our farm. I glanced at my brother. He wore an odd smile.

"See it?" I asked, turning my attention back toward the creature. It lifted off the branch at that moment and began a slow, lazy arc in our direction. As it drew nearer, I could tell it was most definitely too big to be a crow.

"Yeah, I see it," my brother answered quietly.

"Way too big for a turkey buzzard or a hawk," I said, transfixed. "But what—" I stopped short as the creature picked up speed. I could hear the faint flapping of its wings, even from this distance. It was the largest bird I'd ever seen.

Settling on top of the fence post closest to the porch, across the driveway, the creature fixed its eyes on ours. I stared hard, trying to figure out what it might be. Ugly, black, and wrinkled, it resembled a giant, hideous bat.

"What an ugly bird," I managed.

"It isn't a bird," my brother murmured, his odd smile still fixed in place.

"Then what?" But, even then, I knew. My brother said nothing. He didn't need to.

My brother had called the creature. I don't know how or when—or where it had come from, for that matter. But he had called it, like he'd said he would. To take care of "Horrible Harriet" for both of us.

We sat there for a very long time, just us and that creature. In the dim light, I could almost make out its face. It was round, like an owl's, and misshapen. At least, I felt certain it was a face. I couldn't really tell.

We had a different teacher the next day at Waterford Elementary School. "A most unfortunate accident," the principal told us as he introduced our new teacher to us.

"Horrible Harriet" had been in a nasty car wreck the previous evening. She'd likely be in the hospital for months. So we were going to have a new teacher, a rumpled, elderly woman who'd taught at the school for years and had agreed to postpone her retirement for another year.

And that, my dear friends, was the first time Jude called on them for something he wanted or felt like he wanted. It seemed so simple. For him, I think it probably was.

# Chapter Two

My editor tossed a magazine and a newspaper on my desk—an old copy of *Forbes* magazine that had my brother's face on it and a copy of today's *New York Post*. There was a faint *swish* as they slid across the surface and settled a few inches from the edge.

"Is it true?" he asked me.

"Is what true?"

"Your brother. Is he running for the US Senate seat in New York? The *Post* has it on page six."

"Based on …?"

"Something someone overheard at a dinner party." My editor shrugged.

"I'm assuming it's an anonymous source?"

"Of course. But I'm standing in front of someone who's in a better position to know and can confirm it for the metro desk."

I glanced down at my brother's face on the cover of the *Forbes* magazine. They'd profiled him years ago with the headline: "Can He Save Us?" At the time, it had merely been a question. Since then, Jude had answered it fairly satisfactorily.

I hadn't talked to my brother much since *Forbes* had put together his profile, which they did shortly after his daring bet that had almost single-handedly saved the dollar on global currency markets. I'd declined to talk to the reporter, but he'd found plenty of other sources for the extraordinarily flattering profile. Countless sycophants surrounded my brother, especially since the *Forbes* cover piece had cemented his reputation within the global business community.

"Couldn't tell you," I answered truthfully. "I haven't talked to him in two years."

"Really?" My editor seemed genuinely surprised.

"Yeah, really."

I hated questions about my brother. Everyone always wanted to know things about him. Did he really bet every single dollar he'd inherited against the Chinese yuan, crashing the currency of the planet's second-biggest economy on the world market and netting him nearly 10 billion in American dollars when the bet went his way? Was it true he'd done it so he could send China's overextended lending institutions into a tailspin, boost the US economy, save the dollar, and then become chairman of the Federal Reserve? Was it true he'd gotten his law degree from Harvard in just two years and his MBA from Stanford in only nine months? Was it true he'd turned down offers to be secretary of the treasury because he was more interested in the presidency?

I always had the same answer: "Ask Jude." I didn't speak for him, and he was more than capable of speaking for himself. In fact, that's what everyone always said about him. Jude was a brilliant, mesmerizing speaker. He could walk into any room with a crowd, big or small, and walk out with a new legion of fans. People hung on his every word. He certainly didn't need me to speak for him.

"Hmmm," said my editor. He pushed his glasses up the bridge of his nose and simply stared at me. John Hargrove was a good guy, and the environment and science reporters he managed at *The New York Times* liked him immensely. I was one of those admirers. Hargrove had always been fair and decent to me, his problem child. But I also knew when he was serious. He didn't have to say anything. I knew what he wanted.

I sighed. "I'll call him and ask. But I want you to know I'm not happy about it. Jude and I do our own thing. I don't see him much, and we hardly ever talk. His world isn't my world. I've tried hard, as you know, to put distance between the two."

"Fine. I understand," Hargrove said. "But you'll get his answer?"

"Yeah, I'll get his answer. But it's gonna cost you …"

Hargrove smiled. "Let me guess. The Arctic trip?"

"Yeah, the Arctic trip. I get his answer, and you put it in the paper. I get permission to go see the ice in the Arctic—what's left of it. I'll put together a piece that you'll be proud of."

"I'm not worried about that. I'm assuming you want time to report on the conditions there?"

"Yeah, I'll need at least two weeks," I answered. "I'll get out to the middle of the sea on one of the oil ships. I've already got the route planned. I can probably catch a ride, and it won't cost the paper much."

The unspoken truth—and Hargrove knew this—was that I could *buy* a ship to carry me to the Arctic. But I'd never operated that way and wouldn't now. I played by the unwritten laws of journalism. I tried my utmost never to cut corners, ethical or otherwise. Hargrove appreciated it. Other editors at the newspaper thought I was a bit out of my mind.

Hargrove thought about it briefly. "I'm not sure I want you taking a free ride on one of the oil company's ships …"

"They're already going that direction. Don't worry. I plan to throw in a bit about the oil they're finding, but my real focus will be the ice."

Hargrove peered down at the *Forbes* magazine cover and then back at me. "All right. You've got a deal. But I want an answer from your brother. If he does this—and I'm assuming he likely will—you and I both know where it will ultimately end up." He strode back toward his windowless office in the interior of the *Times* building.

That was one of the things I admired about Hargrove. He'd opted for a smaller, less glamorous office, so he could hang out with the reporting staff who worked out of cubicles.

I knew today's deal hadn't been a tough call for him. I'd been lobbying him for weeks to be able to get up to the Arctic to report on the sea-ice situation and what it meant for the planet. Most likely, he'd been ready to cave in to my relentless pursuit of the story, so confirming my brother's plan to run for the Senate was a convenient quid pro quo for him.

I actually had to pull out my cell phone to search for Jude's personal number. I literally hadn't called him in two years—not since the incident that had nearly ended our relationship and severed all family ties.

I found his number and dialed.

Surprisingly, Jude answered before it went to voice mail. "I knew you'd call," he said without preamble.

"My editor asked me to," I replied coldly.

"Sure, whatever," Jude said lightly. "Still, I'm glad you called. I've wanted to talk to you about this. I think it makes sense, but I wanted your advice on what the media will think of it, how they'll play it. This is a necessary stepping stone, but it can go sideways if I'm not careful."

I closed my eyes. If I'd been a religious person—which, surprisingly, given everything I'd learned over the years, I wasn't—I'd have said a quick prayer to God. But no prayer emerged. I opened my eyes and forged ahead. "I guess it was simply a matter of time. You've done everything else. Politics may as well be next up on the Jude World Adventure Tour."

I could almost see my brother smiling on the other end of the line. "You know me better than anyone, Thomas. You always have."

"Yes, I suppose. But what advice could I possibly offer? I'm sure you've studied this from every conceivable angle. You always do. You always have."

"Yes, I have. But I'm concerned that some in the media might look at this as a diversion—or worse, as an ill-advised effort to buy a seat in the Senate."

"So?" I snorted. "Like you'd care. Others have done precisely that. Bloomberg ran for office with his own money. So have others. If you have the money, you can spend it. The Supreme Court has already given billionaires like you the right to spend whatever you want to get the national government you want—"

"Calm down, brother," Jude said. "We're not talking about that here, and you know it. I don't intend to buy an election for someone else."

"You intend to buy it for yourself."

"Sure, if need be," he answered calmly. "But the real question is whether it makes sense to do this right now, not how I actually accomplish it. That's merely a detail."

I had to laugh. "Yeah, a minor detail, the democratic process."

Jude ignored me. "So how will the media play it? Will they get it? I need them to take this seriously. It's important."

I shook my head. I knew Jude already had the answers to the questions he was asking. He was only looking for validation from me, as always.

"Seriously?" I said. "You're asking me how the media will play the story? You know *precisely* how they'll play it—that you'll become a senator and then use it almost immediately as a platform for higher office after that. Unlike me, every other reporter on the planet adores you and follows you around like a puppy—the blunt, straight-talking Jude Asher, who doesn't pull punches, takes enormous personal and professional risks, and always tells it like it is. How could the media not swing in behind the story line? It's scripted perfectly. Even your enemies, if you had any, would get it."

"Good, good," Jude said. "I thought as much. But it's great to hear it from you. You have a sense for these things. You've always had that gift, knowing a good story when you find it. It's why you're a great reporter. It's why you'll win a Pulitzer Prize one of these days for all your 'save the planet' nonsense—"

I cut him off. "I'm not trying to save the planet. It'll be fine. I'm trying to save us, the human species. And I'm not a great reporter, but I'm not sure where else to be or even what to do. Most of my colleagues have no idea why I'm here."

"Because of the inheritance and the wealth? The fact that you're—"

"Yeah, of course," I snapped. "They're not stupid. They have a general idea what we're worth—what both of us are worth even if I have separated myself from you and the business. They'd all kill to have what I—what *we*—got from our adoptive parents and from all of your business ventures, bets, and efforts."

"Not only my efforts," Jude murmured. "You were right there with me, brother, every step of the way ..."

Somehow we ended up here in every conversation. I was tired of it. I'd been tired of it for as long as I could remember. There was nothing I could do to change Jude's mind, and I wanted no part of his approach to life. He'd chosen his path. I'd long ago decided that I'd find something else to pursue, something that didn't intersect with Jude's world.

"Yeah, okay," I said curtly. "So I can tell my editor that it's true? You're running for Senate?"

"Yes, it's true," he admitted, "and I hope you'll join me, join the campaign effort. It would be good to see you again, to work together—like we used to before your inexplicable decision."

"I have my own life, Jude," I threw in tersely. "It doesn't revolve around yours. Not now, not ever."

"As you wish, brother," he said gently. "But you'll at least show up for the campaign announcement? You'll give me that? You're the only family I have, Thomas. It's only the two of us, especially now our adoptive parents are gone. It's always been just the two of us against the others."

"Yeah, and I think the others got the short end of the stick," I said in a wry tone. "I'd never bet against you, no matter how many they line up on the other side."

"Ha! There's the brother I know."

"You may not know me as well as you think. I'm trying to see if I can't give back a little."

Jude laughed. "Good for you. You tell me how that works out for you and the rest of the world. But right now, can I count on you at the campaign appearance? It'll be fun. I think the setting will surprise you."

"Nothing about you surprises me anymore, Jude. You, of all people, should know that. You may have others fooled. But not me."

"So you'll be there?" he pressed.

"You really need me there?"

"I wouldn't ask if I didn't," Jude said. "And honestly—at least to the political cognoscenti who follow these things closely—it would just raise more questions than you'd care to answer if you weren't there. I think you can probably see that for yourself, given the newspaper you work for."

"Okay, yeah, sure. I'll be there," I grumbled. "But I'm not saying anything on your behalf. Please don't ask me to say anything nice about you publicly. Not now or ever. You might not like what I'd say."

"Thanks, brother." He chuckled. "Glad you're in—and I'm glad you called. It's been far too long. See you soon."

I hung up and almost jumped out of my chair. I truly didn't know what to do about my brother. I had no idea. And if I were honest, I'd never known. He'd made up his mind, and there was no pushing him from the path.

I moved through the *Times'* newsroom quickly, toward my editor's office, and walked in without knocking. "It's true," I reported. "He's running."

"And we can attribute it to him?"

"Yeah, Jude Asher, the billionaire investor and former chairman of the Federal Reserve, confirmed to *The New York Times* that he's running for Senate in New York. You get one guess what he plans to do after that."

Hargrove grinned. "I guess he didn't have anything better to do right now?"

"Apparently not." I turned to leave. "Okay, I'm out. You'll see me in two weeks. I'm going up to the top of the world to see if they have any polar bears left. I'll send you a postcard."

"I'd better see more than a postcard," Hargrove growled.

"Don't worry. You will."

# Chapter Three

It was only a different type of game to him at first. But, not surprisingly, it became more as he grew accustomed to it. Jude wasn't satisfied to just call on forces—he wanted to learn how to use his mind to get other people to bend to his will. I think he enjoyed the mind games even more than his ability to call on outside forces to get what he wanted.

"You worry too much," Jude told me. "What's the worst that can happen? We get kicked down the road to yet another foster home? It's not like anyone would believe us or even care. They don't punish you for your thoughts or what you tell people."

"I know, but …"

"But what? Do they have mind police sitting around telling us what we can think and what we can't? What we say? Of course not. We can think whatever we'd like. We can wish for anything we'd like. We can daydream about anything we'd like. No one can keep us from doing that. They're just thoughts. It's the actions that matter."

Jude won these arguments. It wasn't like I could counter them. I certainly couldn't *see* anything around us that would keep us from wondering and thinking about the things Jude talked about.

By the time we were in middle school, we were already on our sixth set of foster parents. Jude had long ago given up on the questions. He no longer cared why no one had adopted us when we were babies. Because that, of course, is the only time kids get adopted. Everyone wants to adopt a baby—a brand-new human being they can raise as their very own and teach to think like them. No one wants kids with their own minds.

And Jude very much had his own unique mind. I did too. But I tended to be a listener, a follower, a scribe of the events around me. Jude was the kid who forged ahead. I tended to follow behind and take his lead.

Jude found creative ways into social circles wherever we landed. He didn't wait to ask questions. Whenever circumstances changed, for whatever reason, he just moved on, did his own thing, won friends, and quietly punished any possible enemies.

Sometimes, for fun, he made suggestions—ones that his highly inventive mind dreamed up—and then sat back to see what would happen. It was his private game.

After our blissful, largely uneventful couple of years with the nice, elderly couple on the farm in Waterford, Virginia, we had to move on yet again.

The man had been an insurance salesman. But he retired after the company he worked for had been crushed by the economic recession in the first decade of the twenty-first century, and the couple had been forced to sell their farm. They moved to a crummy one-bedroom apartment in the closest town—which, of course, left no room for us.

We went back into the system, which spit us out and landed us with a family that somehow managed to jam ten kids into a townhouse in Purcellville, Virginia. Four of the kids were their biological children. They split two of the bedrooms on the top floor of the townhouse. The six foster kids, including us, slept on pullout beds in the basement.

Jude said this particular set of foster parents paid for the townhouse from what the state gave them to take care of us. I'm sure he was right. What I never could quite figure was why the state let so many kids stay in that townhouse. Maybe they decided it was better than shipping us off to some institution.

Jude didn't care. "It is what it is," he said. And we certainly weren't given a chance to ask anyone that question. The state could be a rather impersonal thing.

By then, I'd already read all the books on foster care. I'd studied them over and over. That was just my nature. I couldn't help it. I knew, for instance, that a lot of your brain development occurs when you're young, like three or four. Without loving parents telling a child what to think, who knew what happened in a just-beginning-to-form brain?

Foster kids have higher suicide rates, higher rates of depression, and a greater chance of getting hooked on drugs. We're worse in school, and we're much more likely to get in trouble. Half of the foster kids in the United States choose to be homeless when they turn eighteen, thinking that it's a better alternative than the lot they'd drawn up to that point.

In fact, a few studies reported that a third of the homeless in America had once been foster kids. I don't know if that's true or not. But Jude said it didn't matter. We were never going to be that sort of statistic, he vowed. We would absolutely control our own destiny. Statistics were just that—statistics.

There was an unspoken hierarchy in the Purcellville foster home. The four teenage kids who belonged to the family, all boys, were in charge. They grabbed fistfuls of french fries at dinner and left the scraps for the rest of us. They took the seats in the Ford truck, leaving the rest of us to hang out in the bed of the truck. They got a ride to school. We took the bus.

Their parents didn't step in. If anything, they seemed to get a perverse pleasure in watching this dynamic. I couldn't even begin to explain the psychology behind it. Someone, somewhere, could probably have come up with an explanation.

"Leave it alone," Jude said once. "It doesn't matter. It's not something we can control—at least not right now."

But I watched Jude with those four boys—and I learned. Jude said he didn't care, that he was ignoring the injustice of it. He claimed to pay no attention to the slights, the taunts, the not-so-subtle threats that if we didn't toe the line and follow along, we'd be out on our own or in an even more horrible foster-care situation.

In practice, though, Jude did something else. Unlike the rest of us foster kids, he adopted a stance of hanging out with the four boys, echoing their words, puffing them up, telling them how wonderful and smart they were. As he became their personal echo chamber, both at the house and in school, the four boys began to cut Jude some slack. But more important, they started listening to his suggestions here and there. I could tell Jude was setting them up, though I couldn't even imagine what form the setup would take.

One night, the entire family of kids—foster and "real" kids alike—watched an old movie. It was the original horror film, one that spawned others in the genre years later. It was supposed to scare the living daylights out of us. One of the other foster kids had heard about it and rented it from the public library. The movie was called *The Bad Seed*. The original was filmed in the 1950s, but it was remade decades later.

I watched Jude while the film played. He smiled and laughed throughout. During a movie that was supposed to be scary—a story about a pretty, adorable little girl who killed friends and neighbors to get what she wanted whenever she wanted. But I could see Jude thought the movie was silly—especially the ending, when a lightning bolt zapped her on the dock of a lake as she looked at the water for a medal her mother had tossed into the murky depths.

"No way," he whispered to me at the end. "No way does that happen in real life."

"Why not?" I asked him.

He frowned. "Because it doesn't work that way. That idiot girl didn't need to kill those people. There are other ways to get what you want. And you don't need to put the janitor in the incinerator to cover your tracks. That's plain stupid."

At the time, we were studying chemistry in middle school. Jude took an uncanny interest in the class, which was unusual for him. He didn't ordinarily put so much work into studying. That was my thing. But there was something about this particular class that fascinated him. I think it had something to do with understanding the fundamental essence of the world, which is what chemistry can teach if one pays attention.

Jude launched his game about six weeks after we'd learned some of the basics of chemistry. It started with another old movie, a western starring Clint Eastwood. Jude spent the entire time talking about how gunpowder had changed everything in the Old West.

"The invention of gunpowder," he said, "was the coolest thing ever.

"What's more," Jude then whispered to one of the biological kids, "we could actually do it ourselves. We could make gunpowder right in our own kitchen."

The boys didn't believe him, of course. But Jude taught them. They concocted the gunpowder themselves and made it right there in the kitchen three days later when their mother was out shopping. Jude made them write down the ingredients themselves and then buy it from the store. He patiently explained the process to them.

Jude then took the four boys to a construction site around the corner. They "borrowed" some of the pipe intended for the interior plumbing and brought it back to the townhouse. Jude showed them how to take the gunpowder and stuff it inside a six-inch pipe, close off the ends, and then put some string in one end.

"Just for fun," Jude suggested, "why not see what happens if you light the end and drop it inside one of the Porta-Johns on the construction site this weekend when no one's around? That would be cool, right? Just see what might happen?"

The four teenagers were suckered in.

It *was* pretty interesting, I had to admit. The pipe exploded inside the Porta-John and blew the sides open in either direction. A fountain of waste exploded a good twenty feet into the air like an erupting geyser. The four boys laughed themselves silly watching it.

Jude simply wore that odd smile again.

"But wouldn't it be even cooler," he suggested to the boys a while later, "to try out the pipe bombs on some of the mailboxes in the neighborhood? To put one inside a mailbox and blow it to smithereens?"

So the four boys took some more gunpowder, filled more pipes, and then fanned out across the neighborhood to target some of the mailboxes of our neighbors.

I watched as Jude faded into the background throughout all of this. I took his lead and stayed in the shadows as well.

The four boys planted the pipes, blew up the mailboxes, and then ran back to the townhouse to talk about the daring effort.

Jude suggested other targets, including one of the blue USPS mailbox drops right outside the 7-Eleven a few blocks from the house.

"What morons," Jude said to me after they'd gone.

"How so?" I asked him.

He shook his head. "Well, for one thing, it's a felony to blow up mailboxes. It's a federal crime. The local paper says that the FBI has already shown up to investigate, along with the local cops. Porta-Johns are one thing. Mailboxes are something else entirely."

I almost gasped. But I had to admit, I was also curious about where this train wreck might end up. "But we're involved, aren't we?"

"No, we're not," Jude said firmly. "They wrote the ingredients down, they bought them from the store, and they took those pipes and stuffed the gunpowder inside. They blew them up at the construction site while we watched. They walked around the neighborhood and put them in the mailboxes—"

"But you gave them the idea," I interrupted. "Doesn't that mean something?"

"Yeah, maybe. But it won't matter after tonight—not after the security camera at the 7-Eleven clearly shows them putting that pipe bomb inside the mailbox. They can squawk all they want about where they got the idea from. They're the morons who'll be on the security camera tape."

And just like clockwork, agents with blue windbreakers that had the letters *FBI* emblazoned across the back showed up the next morning. They sat down with the four boys and their parents to explain what they'd seen on the camera. They sternly announced that it was a federal crime to blow up mailboxes and warned that the four boys could have been sent away for the rest of their natural lives as domestic terrorists if they'd been eighteen years old.

The four boys did everything they could to pin it on Jude. They squealed like stuck pigs—telling the FBI agents that Jude was the mastermind behind the effort, teaching them how to make the gunpowder, showing them where to find the pipe, suggesting the targets.

Jude sat there calmly throughout his interrogation. He didn't deny anything but calmly and very directly pointed out to the FBI agents that they'd all taken chemistry class together and that he'd never made the gunpowder, never stolen pipe from the construction site, never blown up anything. And, he noted, he wasn't on the security camera either. As far as he knew, Jude said, it wasn't a crime to listen to other people.

Granted, Jude knew it *was* a crime to be an accomplice. But I think he also knew it would be nearly impossible for the FBI to pursue that course of action, given that Jude had done nothing more than plant a suggestion here and there. Jude's fingerprints, so to speak, were nowhere to be found. The four boys, on the other hand, were caught red-handed, and no amount of squealing could erase that plain, simple fact.

In the end, the FBI concluded the same thing. They threatened to send the four boys—not Jude—off to juvenile detention for some period of time but ultimately decided against it after long consultations with the parents and several lawyers.

The four boys had been scared straight. They wouldn't wander off the path ever again. They'd graduate from high school and safely fold themselves into crummy jobs and dull lives. They would never take risks again, and the FBI agents would continue to haunt their dreams.

But not Jude. The whole thing had been an experiment for him—one of many mind games—to see if words alone could move antagonists out of the way. They could. He'd learned an interesting, valuable lesson. You could sometimes get your way, get what you want, simply by talking. It was a very curious thing.

And he'd been able to do so with his own mind, without calling on outside forces. In this case, at least, it hadn't been necessary.

The parents shipped us off to yet another foster home within two months of the incident. Jude may have fooled the FBI, but the parents had a pretty clear idea about the true mastermind behind it all.

Jude didn't care, and I didn't really care either. I was ready to move on again. I'd long ago resigned myself to both my fate in life and the fact that I would go where Jude took me. I was inextricably tied to Jude. It didn't seem like I had much of a choice in the matter.

## CHAPTER FOUR

My third girlfriend in five years was perplexed. We'd been planning a vacation to the Caribbean for the past couple of months, and I was postponing it to take the trip up north after I made my cameo appearance at the launch of Jude's Senate campaign.

"You're going to the Arctic ocean at this time of year, in the summer?" she whispered fiercely over her nonfat, sugar-free grande mocha coffee in the Starbucks on Madison Avenue near her office. "Why?"

Sandy was a nice young woman, an executive vice president of a decent-sized advertising agency with some A-list corporate clients. She worked hard, played even harder, and had a social network in the city to kill for. She just had lousy taste in boyfriends, she would occasionally remind me.

"It's the time to go," I offered lamely. "They're going to record the lowest level of sea ice in history—"

"Yeah, so? I read that story. I know, because I read it already this summer in *The New York Times*. And I'm pretty sure it had your byline."

"It did," I said, "but no one gets the importance up there. They don't understand what it means. It isn't just about the area that the ice covers; it's about the volume. A British researcher predicted twenty years ago that we'd see the Arctic sea ice disappear in our lifetime, not by the end of the century. And he was right."

I was on a roll. "Have you seen the PIOMAS charts for the last twenty years? The NASA satellites can only look down on the surface area. They can't pick up the cubic volume. I have to explain the difference between volume and ice cover, so people will understand why it's fundamentally altering the jet stream and affecting extreme weather events like drought, heat waves, and storm surges ..."

I stopped speaking. I could see I'd lost her already. I did that often with her, especially when I was focused on something—like right now and the meaning behind the situation in the Arctic.

I cocked my head. "It was the PIOMAS chart, wasn't it?"

"PIOMAS? Seriously?" She tucked a strand of shoulder-length blonde hair behind her right ear.

I hurried on. "Well, it's important. These researchers at the University of Washington have been trying to guess the volume of ice being lost each year in the Arctic Ocean because of the extreme warming happening there. PIOMAS stands for—"

"I don't *care* what it stands for!" Her voice rose a decibel. "That's not the point. And I'm sure it's important. But we've been planning to go to the Caribbean, and I already scheduled my vacation around my clients."

"Can't you reschedule?"

She exhaled dramatically. "I could, but not without moving heaven and earth. That's why we planned it, so I wouldn't have to go through this."

I looked at her. We were right there at the edge of the boyfriend cliff. I'd been at the edge of that cliff many times over the years. I always walked right off the edge. And I was about to do it again.

It was a shame. Sandy was a really nice person. She was fun to be with. We seemed to like the same things. We could both go see the Yankees play and delight when they lost. We'd both rather see an off-Broadway play with struggling actors than *The Book of Mormon*. We enjoyed the flea market on Amsterdam Avenue on Saturdays.

And we both loved the fact that we were infinitely more comfortable reading the *Times* at a coffee shop on Sunday morning than sitting in a church pew.

But—and I think Sandy knew this—I was always holding back. I never truly talked about anything of substance around her—or anyone else for that matter. How could I tell anyone what I'd seen in my life?

Sandy was so nice, in fact, that she'd never even asked about my inheritance, the wealth, or why I was working at the *Times* as an environmental science reporter when I didn't need to. I was pretty sure she'd read stories about Jude and me over the years. She could fill in the blanks. But she didn't ask outright, which was another thing I liked about her.

Yet I wondered if it would ever work with us. Sandy didn't want to go too deeply into the world. She liked to skate on the surface, and she was awfully good at it. She could dance, twirl, and socialize with the best of them. And me? I was profoundly uncomfortable on the surface. The smoldering fire and intensity of my life hovered beneath that surface, waiting to devour anyone who came too close.

"I have to go," I said finally.

Her hazel eyes pierced mine. "You don't have to go. You *want* to."

"I've been lobbying my editor for weeks to cover this story in more depth. You know that. I've told you about it."

"Sure, but why do you have to go now? Why can't you wait a bit? Do it later in the year, after our vacation?"

"The ships are all sailing there. It's now or never," I added half-heartedly. There was some truth in this, but not enough to convince her, I knew.

"Whatever." Sandy pushed her chair back from the table at Starbucks, grabbed her cup of coffee, and rose to leave. "I may not know what a PIOMAS chart is, but I do know this: I'm going on my vacation with or without you."

"Sandy, please—"

"I'm serious," she said firmly. "You know I am. If you go to the Arctic, I can't promise I'll even return your phone call when you get back."

She waited for a few more moments to see if I'd relent. When I didn't, she turned and stalked out. I thought briefly about calling after her, telling her that, all right, I'd go on vacation with her to the Caribbean.

But I didn't. Instead I chose to let the boyfriend cliff take a victim yet again.

# Chapter Five

I never quite understood why Jude never worried about anything. He just didn't. Somewhere along the line, I think, Jude simply decided that the world had thrown its worst at him, and he'd absorbed it. Now he meant to deal with the world as he wanted, as he saw fit, and he didn't care what anyone else thought. He was the master of his own fate.

There is a certain freedom in not caring what others think about you. Don't get me wrong—Jude went out of his way to cultivate a circle of people who considered him a friend or acquaintance. But they weren't really *his* friends or acquaintances. They were props. And he truly didn't care what they thought—about him or anything else.

"Why do you worry so much?" he once asked me. "How does it help? What does it get you? Does it make our situation better? Does it bring us parents who love us, a family that supports us? No. So there's no need to worry. Just get on with it, and do everything that's under your control."

"But life *isn't* under our control," I'd countered. "We're trapped by our circumstances. There are things that happen to us that we can't control."

"So control it. Take charge of your own destiny, and quit worrying about everything that's outside your own control."

"But we can't," I'd pleaded. "No one can. Things happen that are outside of us, outside of anything that we can directly control."

"Yeah?" Jude had said. "Well, for those instances that we can't directly control, then it becomes necessary to bring other forces into play that can extend your reach."

"That's crazy. Even those things can't keep truly awful circumstances away from you. They can't protect you."

"Why not?"

"Okay," I'd offered. "Let's say a family is driving along at night, minding its own business, and some drunk guy veers over the center line and smashes into them. Everyone dies. Tell me how that family could have controlled that situation."

Jude had shrugged. "That's easy. If I was part of that family, there's no way that drunk guy hits our car. Not now. It wouldn't happen. Those *things*—as you occasionally refer to them—would make sure I was protected."

"How?"

Jude smiled his knowing smile. "The drunk guy would overcorrect at the last minute, right before he hit us. He'd yank the wheel back in the other direction viciously, careen off the side of the road on the other side of us, flip his car, and smash himself into a million pieces. We'd drive on, unscathed."

"And those … protectors, or whatever you call them, would take care of that? They'd make sure that drunk guy turned away?"

"If it's a question of him or me, and I called on them to make that choice, then, yes, that's what would happen. That which you demand is yours."

"As opposed to 'Ask, and you shall receive'?"

"No need to ask," he'd said. "There's only one way to make absolutely certain you get what you want."

At some point, I quit arguing with Jude about this sort of thing, largely because he was telling the truth as he saw it. Somewhere along the way, Jude *did* start to learn how to control circumstances beyond himself when the need arose. What he demanded, he got.

My first understanding was early in our high school years. We were freshmen at our second high school, living with our eighth set of foster parents. Neither of us knew how long we'd be with this set of foster parents or at this particular high school. But I knew, right off, that Jude wouldn't sit still for very long at the bottom of the social heap.

Jude hated everything about that setup—being a freshman, I mean. He hated hierarchies with a passion. And that's what high school was—a hierarchy, with freshmen at the bottom. It was only later that he decided to stop fighting them and just rise to the top of those in his path.

It was much worse for boys than for girls—at least for the cute girls. If you were a freshman girl, and you were pretty, then you had little trouble socially. You had lots of friends, and the older boys in high school flitted around you like hummingbirds. It was so wonderful, nice, and delicious for the cute freshman girls. They simply had to be themselves, smile, flirt, be coy and cute, and their social network expanded exponentially.

Jude and I, on the other hand, were almost instantly relegated to the social-outcast wing of high school, along with most of the freshmen boys. We had barely any hope of talking to—much less dating—any of the cute freshmen girls. Sophomore, junior, and senior girls, of course, were off-limits. And had we been interested in sports, we'd have run into much the same thing—those who were older than us ruled and served as captains and commanders of their various teams by virtue of their birth dates and nothing more.

Jude had seen enough of this after a couple of weeks.

"We need to change things up," he said mysteriously. "Time to burn the social order to the ground. Literally."

It was an ordinary Friday-night party at someone's house at the end of a suburban cul-de-sac. Word had spread, as it generally did when kids gathered at McDonald's. Parents gone for the weekend, kid left home alone, and a party was born.

Jude talked me into joining him in attending, against my wishes. I knew I'd likely spend the party hanging out at the fringes, unable to talk to anyone. It would be miserable.

"Upstairs," he said when we arrived. "I want to see the layout of the house."

I lifted an eyebrow. "Why?"

"You'll see."

We worked our way through throngs of kids gathered at the bottom of the stairwell. I knew what we'd find upstairs, and it wasn't pretty. I recognized at least six of the cute freshmen girls who were in various close encounters. I'd never talked to any of them, but I recognized them.

"Okay, good," Jude said after he'd walked through each of the bedrooms on the upper level of the modest suburban house. Jude paused for a bit at the last room, what looked like an alcove storage room that had been converted into a fourth bedroom. There were two freshman girls—and the two upper-class boys they were making out with—inside this fourth bedroom. He was thoughtful as he closed the door behind us on the way out.

I couldn't help but be puzzled. "What's good about any of that?"

"The way the house is laid out," he explained. "That last room, the alcove storage room with the two freshman girls, is perfect. The door only locks one way, from the outside, from the hallway. It clearly used to be a storage closet and only locks with a key. And there are no windows in the room itself. They'll be trapped there when the smoke starts."

"Smoke? What in the world—"

Jude held up a hand. "Relax. It'll make sense. Just follow my lead when it's time."

Had I known what Jude had planned—what he'd already set in motion by calling on his forces—I would most certainly *not* have followed Jude's lead. Had I known that he was planning to call on forces to actually threaten people lives simply for better social status, I would never have played along. But by the time I'd realized what he was up to, I didn't have much choice.

I trailed behind Jude as he worked his way back downstairs. He didn't say a word to a soul at the party. He was grimly determined to some as-yet-unexplained task. He went to the kitchen and looked around, spotted a number of key rings hanging beside the refrigerator, grabbed one, and then headed back upstairs.

Once we were back upstairs, Jude rummaged through a closet at the end of the hall until he found what he was looking for. He pulled two blankets out of the closet, handed one to me, then joined the line outside the one and only upstairs bathroom. But he quickly grew impatient at the wait.

"Follow me," he urged.

I did. We went back down the stairs a second time and made our way outside. Jude walked around the hedges and bushes at the side of the house until he spotted a green hose. He grabbed the end of the hose and turned on the water.

"Put your blanket on the ground," he ordered. He tossed his blanket on the ground beside mine and doused both with water, then switched the water off. Reaching down, he started to wring some of the water out of his blanket. Not knowing precisely why I was doing it, I followed his lead and wrung the water out of my blanket. We left the blankets slightly damp.

We walked back into the house and up the stairs yet again. Jude glanced around and, satisfied at what he saw, took the set of keys he'd brought with him from the kitchen, chose the one labeled "upstairs bedroom," locked the door from the outside, and stepped back.

"Showtime," he said enigmatically.

We waited for a minute or two before we heard the shouts coming from the kitchen below, followed by even more shouts, then screams of terror, and finally, the word that Jude was clearly waiting to hear.

"Fire!" someone yelled, racing out of the kitchen. "The house is on fire! Get out!"

Mass hysteria ensued. Every kid pushed and shoved to get down the stairs and out of the now-burning house. Doors slammed. Windows were smashed. Smoke—lots and lots of it—billowed out of the kitchen in black streams. Within a minute or so, all of that black smoke had created a haze upstairs.

Jude waited calmly at the end of the long hallway, outside the room he'd locked moments earlier. He positioned himself so he could see the downstairs living room as well. As the smoke and cries of terror reached the bedrooms, I heard pounding from the other side of that locked door.

"Let us out! Let us out!" one of the freshmen girls screamed from the other side of the locked door. I could hear the boys on the other side pounding frantically. Smoke billowed heavily. It was getting hard to breathe. I wondered if perhaps Jude hadn't turned loose something that he couldn't control.

Jude didn't react until the first licks of the fire emerged from the kitchen and caught the drapes in the living room. Then he moved into action. He grabbed the wet blanket and motioned to me to grab mine.

"Remember—follow my lead," he hissed. Jude unlocked the door, turned the knob, and crashed through the door as violently as he could manage. The swinging door knocked one of the two boys over as we raced into the bedroom. The smoke billowed upstairs, thick and hazy all around us.

"I have you!" Jude called to one of the girls. He took his wet blanket, wrapped it around the girl, and started to lead her out of the room. I followed Jude's lead and wrapped the second girl in my own wet blanket.

Jude looked over at me, his eyes blazing cauldrons of intensity, saw that I had my prize, and then charged back out of the room. "Let's go!" he yelled. "Follow me!" He held on to the girl in his arms, inside the wet blanket, and hurried through the smoke and down the stairs. We followed as swiftly as we could.

We ran through the small but growing blaze of fire and smoke that was rapidly enveloping the living room.

All six of us raced out of the house and joined the group of kids gathered on the front lawn. They stood watching the inferno take over the house.

"You saved my life!" the girl told Jude. He unwrapped the wet blanket from around her as we reached the safety of the front lawn. She collapsed into Jude's arms, sobbing uncontrollably.

"I can't believe you risked your lives like that," someone said in awe.

"Yeah, you brought them out of that burning house," said a second.

"You're heroes," said a third.

Word spread quickly about the two freshmen boys who'd risked their lives to save the four kids trapped in an upstairs bedroom during a raging fire. We were no longer faceless freshmen in a hierarchical world ruled by birthright elders. We had status, thanks to Jude.

People love heroes. Becoming one changes everything about your life and your world almost instantly. Jude and I were no longer at the bottom of the heap. No, at least for now, for as long as we were in that particular high school, we were afforded a different social ranking.

Just as Jude had planned.

# Chapter Six

The park had been unoccupied for quite some time when my brother arrived in force to announce his campaign. I appreciated the irony. I'm not sure anyone else did.

The Occupy Wall Street movement had been on the cusp of redefining American politics once. Fueled by the anger at the "1 percent"—the people like my brother (and yes, myself) who commanded unseemly amounts of wealth compared to the other 99 percent of the American population who lived paycheck to paycheck—the movement had begun in New York at Battery Park in the shadow of the Twin Towers and then spread from city to city across America.

And then, in the blink of an eye, it had largely gone away. Unlike the Arab Spring revolutionary movements that had unseated governments around the world—and continued to disrupt democracies in those same countries—the Occupy Wall Street movement had gradually become a distant memory for the fickle national media.

The beginning of the end came as winter approached Battery Park at the southern end of Manhattan, when Mayor Bloomberg—a card-carrying 1-percenter himself, despite his populist tendencies as a politician—brought in the police to arrest the protesters there and tear down the "city" that had grown on the city block.

What had once been a staging ground for protests, news blasts, clarion calls, and various media targets on the steps of Battery Park by the folks who used the Occupy Wall Street movement for their own purposes once again became a tourist attraction for folks wishing nothing more than to eat their Burger King hamburgers as they stared up at the new tower that had been built on the site of the greatest terrorist tragedy in US history.

As I arrived at Battery Park, however, I couldn't help but marvel at how iconic the location still was. My brother was a genius. If he could pull off his Senate campaign launch from here, the locus of populist protest against the uber-wealthy in American society, then he could achieve almost anything.

The word had clearly gotten around. The park was jammed with curious onlookers, tourists, potential campaign volunteers, well-wishers, and of course, the usual New York street crowd that drifted anywhere action appeared.

But there was also a number of police in riot gear spread around the park. I wasn't entirely sure what they expected, but it was obvious they didn't want to be surprised by anything.

I was surprised at the bank of cameras that had shown up for the campaign announcement. There were already three tiers of cameras directly in front of the podium. I counted at least fifty cameras total. All of the national broadcast networks were there.

*Seriously?* I thought. Jude was running for Senate, not for grand emperor and pooh-bah of the known universe. If he won, he'd be one of one hundred senators, all of whom harbored thoughts of running for president someday … merely one of many in the nation's capital vying for power and attention.

But I also knew Jude's race wasn't ordinary. There were only a few big states in the US—New York, California, Massachusetts, Florida, Illinois, and Texas—capable of producing a governor or senator who could go after the White House at some point.

And Jude clearly had it all—wealth, fame, charisma, and a track record of facing down big, daunting challenges. He only had to turn it into a platform that people could get behind—and deliver something tangible if he did manage to win the Senate seat.

"Over here, Thomas!" a voice called out over the din that filled the park.

I looked up. My brother stood behind a wall of people, all seemingly talking to him at once.

But Jude, at that moment, ignored them and looked down directly at me. Our eyes locked. In the middle of a sea of humanity in one of New York's most crowded, historic, and iconic places, it was just the two of us. I could deny it as much as I'd like, but I couldn't truly avoid the truth.

I smiled grimly, waved, and edged my way up the steps through the crowd. I paused at the solid wall of police at the edge of the makeshift platform where the podium rested and explained who I was to one of them. I was prepared to argue my case, but Jude appeared by my side.

"He's my twin brother. Can't you tell?" Jude said to the policeman. He pulled me close and positioned me so we were both facing him—and the wall of still photographers who'd been milling around.

In one instant, which I'm sure Jude had mapped out thoroughly in advance, because he might never get another opportunity like this with me—not since my decision to separate our lives—a hundred camera flashes went off as the photographers captured the unusual occasion in front of the square.

The cop smiled. "Wow, he's a dead ringer for you, Mr. Asher."

"Yeah, and he's a Mr. Asher too." Jude smiled broadly.

"Just not as famous," I muttered. I leaned over and whispered in my brother's ear. "Get me out of here, Jude. You promised. I don't want a public profile here."

"No worries. I only wanted to make sure you arrived on the platform safely."

Grabbing my shoulder, he guided me up to the row of seats behind the platform and podium. He directed me to a seat slightly off center enough from the podium that I would still be in every single TV camera angle whether I liked it or not. But I didn't care any longer. It was out of my control at this point.

I stopped him right before I sat down. "Are *they* here? *Those things?*"

Jude smiled. "Yes, they are. Always. But you know that."

I glanced around. It had been easier to tell when I was younger. Now, as Jude had gotten more sophisticated and worldly, so had the forces he depended on for help when he called on them. "But where would they be?" I asked. "There are thousands of people. They could be anywhere at all in this crowd."

"Precisely," he said before focusing on the business at hand.

As I watched the crowd settle in for the announcement, I had to marvel again at the scene that Jude had created for it. Off to the right was the site of the World Trade Center that had come down more than a decade earlier, only to be rebuilt again. I was certain that, at some point, Jude would gesture skyward toward that newest tower and remind everyone about the incident—and how it had changed the country.

Behind us, in the park itself, Jude had brought in hundreds of union workers and former members of the Occupy Wall Street movement who were there to say, with their physical presence, that the unions and the 99 percent supported the Democratic nominee for the Senate seat in New York even though he had, in fact, been a literal Wall Street banker once when he was the chairman of the Federal Reserve.

And on stage with us were a whole slew of prominent celebrities who lived in their 20-million-dollar, three-bedroom apartments overlooking the Hudson River, as well as wealthy New York cognoscenti who would undoubtedly raise whatever it took to bankroll his campaign beyond what Jude himself was prepared to spend. Jude's wife was in the front row.

It was curious. Democrats had to be populists and still raise vast sums of money to run for gubernatorial and Senate offices. Very few could manage the trick. Clearly, my brother seemed to have the gift.

I looked off to the side and spotted one of my colleagues from *The New York Times* leaning up against a post, watching the drama in order to report on the campaign announcement. I felt instantly uncomfortable, sitting on the stage as a prop for my brother when my instinct, my real responsibility, was to be off to the side as an observer and scribe. I grimaced at my colleague and rolled my eyes heavenward. He shook his head but grinned back. *At least I'll have a decent campaign source*, I could almost hear him thinking from off in the distance.

The crowd settled to a low roar as the warm-up act stepped up to the microphone on the podium. I hardly even listened to my brother's bio as she read it for the crowd. I knew his story by heart. I certainly didn't need to listen to some stranger recite the public details.

As Jude accepted the introduction and stepped up to the microphone, I noticed that one of the police officers around the podium platform started to rock back and forth rhythmically. He was directly in front of the stage. He was close enough to the stage that Jude and I were both in his line of sight.

It was odd. All the other cops were clearly on edge because of the setting and the big crowd, but they were motionless, only their eyes scanning the crowd. A few occasionally turned to glance at the stage, but this particular cop swayed back and forth. He seemed distracted. He kept turning to look back directly at my brother and me.

As Jude started into his speech about an America capable of rising up from the ashes of defeat to straddle the world again, the words became fuzzy for me. I couldn't take my eyes off the cop. There was something so out of place with him that I couldn't turn away.

When he turned and pulled his revolver from his holster, I reacted instinctively. In an instant, I knew. Like Bobby Kennedy and others in a long line of populist political figures, my brother had become a target for a lone madman intent on taking his infamous place in history.

With time nearly at a standstill, I jumped from my chair behind the podium. We were both in his line of fire, so I took the direct route toward him. I grabbed Jude's shoulder as I rushed by him, pushed hard to force him down behind the podium, and then sprinted past. I covered the last ten feet in a rush and leaped toward the gunman.

He got off only one shot. I could feel the bullet tear through my leg, and then I was on him. I smashed into him like he was a tackling dummy on a practice football field. We crashed to the ground hard. Ignoring any thought of pain or my own personal safety, I grabbed his shooting arm and smashed it to the ground. The gun rattled away.

The rest of the cops were on us a second later, pinning both of us to the ground. I could see two of the cops securing the gun, and two more pinning the shooter to the ground. But a half dozen other cops, not sure exactly what had happened, were literally piling on top of me to keep me in my place.

The intense pain started then. I could feel myself slipping into unconsciousness. There was no keeping it away, and the crowd of police pinning me down wasn't helping matters.

Somehow, through the madness, I heard Jude's voice. "Let him up! Let him up!" he called out from somewhere on the other side of the pile of cops who had me pinned to the pavement. "That's my brother, and he just saved my life."

And then my world went black.

# Chapter Seven

I don't know how long I was out. It could have been an hour or two weeks. All I know was that my brother was standing there, staring down at me balefully when I finally came to after the shooting.

I glanced around the room. I was in some sort of a private hospital recovery room. It was just the two of us.

"Wow, was that dumb." Jude shook his head sadly. "You might at least have told me before pulling a stunt like that. If you recall, that's our deal. We give each other a heads-up before jumping into the hero business."

"It is *not* our deal," I tossed back. "It hasn't been for some time." My eyelids were half open. Excruciating pain radiated up one side of my body, originating from a spot on one of my legs. Then I remembered. I'd been shot by a policeman.

"It is," Jude insisted. "I've always given you fair warning before incidents like that happen."

I tried to sit up, grimaced, and then collapsed back onto the hospital bed. "Yeah, but you plan them, maybe even control them in some weird way I'll never understand."

"You understand, Thomas," he said softly. "You can pretend otherwise, if it makes you feel better. But you understand. You always have."

I didn't answer. I wasn't about to give my brother the satisfaction of knowing that I understood him and how he moved through the world. "So, all right, what's the deal? What happened?"

"You got shot."

"I know that, you moron. What I meant was, why? I thought you had that kind of stuff under control. You told me they were around in droves. So how did something like that happen?"

Jude's eyes bored into mine. "They were around. The event was very well attended. I made certain of that."

"Then how could that have happened? I mean, I'm assuming the guy who tried to shoot you wasn't actually a policeman?"

"No, he wasn't. His name is Samuel Chambers, and he's a religious fanatic."

"So I'll ask again, how? I thought *they* controlled things like that, to keep threats to you away?"

Jude took a deep breath. "I'm still learning, even now. And what I learned there is that anger and hate, once embedded, can't be controlled. Not entirely. Not perfectly. I thought it could. I made assumptions, and I'd received certain assurances. But I was wrong."

"So that guy was like an unguided missile, aimed in certain directions that aren't entirely under anyone's control? And on this particular day, it happened to be aimed at you? And you weren't made aware of this fact?"

Jude's face was a grim mask, holding back a certain fury. "Yeah, something like that. He clearly had a target in mind. There are always random, uncontrolled chances and circumstances at any given time, no matter how well prepared we might be. Humans have free will, after all, up to a point. But that should not have happened. What I don't know, yet, is *why* it happened. Trust me, I intend to find out."

My eyes met my brother's, and our gaze held for a minute in silence. He and I hadn't spoken of this sort of thing in any form or fashion in two years. Our separation had been irrevocable and, I believed, complete. I wasn't even sure I wanted to know any of this any longer. But I couldn't help myself, given what had just happened.

"Come on!" I waved a hand in frustration. "I know you have the ability to direct things. How many times have I seen it?"

"This was different," Jude said sharply. "I didn't direct this. And I don't know, exactly, why it happened. There are some things I don't understand, at least not yet."

"But you have an inkling?"

"Yeah, I have an inkling," he murmured. "But it's a bit like trying to guess what shape might be casting a shadow. I can see the shadow, and I know what's behind it. But I can't see the shape. Someone not under my influence or control wanted something. What I don't know yet was what that might be or why."

"Who? I've always assumed you knew …"

Jude exhaled audibly. He looked at the hospital floor for a minute before he spoke again. "I don't know everything, Thomas. There are a very great many of forces at play at any given time, at quite a few levels. It's not unlike the levels of government that the world knows so well. Some rule little towns. Some rule nations. And some, somehow, rule worlds."

I closed my eyes and rested, still feeling the pain shoot up my leg. "Well," I said slowly, "all I can say is that I hope you didn't plan this—to put me in harm's way, I mean."

"I didn't plan this, Thomas. I would never do that. I give you my word. And you know that means something."

I did. Jude was many things, but a pathological liar wasn't one of them. He'd always been brutally honest and straightforward with me about what he was doing and why. That was something I'd never had to doubt about him.

I scanned the sparse hospital room. I was still struggling to get my bearings. "How long was I out, by the way?"

Jude reached behind him and grabbed something. He plopped a copy of *The New York Times* on my chest. "They gave you a sedative to help you sleep. For your scrapbook. This is the front page of today's paper."

I looked down at the front page, which was covered by an enormous photo. I turned the paper so I could see it more clearly. Someone had snapped a picture of me an instant after I'd taken the bullet in the leg, as I was lunging toward the attacker, who had just fired a shot at my brother, the political candidate.

"Oh no." I groaned. "Seriously? It's on the front page of my own newspaper?"

"Not just your paper," Jude said, laughing. "It's on the front page of every newspaper in the country and half of the papers around the world." He pulled a sheaf of call slips from his shirt pocket. "What's more, you now have, like, two hundred requests for interviews. Every TV producer on the planet wants to book you."

"Great," I muttered. "That sure blows my cover."

"Yep," Jude said. "You're the hero, the guy who thwarted a political assassination attempt."

"And I'll bet it didn't hurt your Senate chances any?"

"It certainly didn't hurt," Jude said ruefully.

"You're absolutely sure you didn't plan this?"

"I meant it before," he said, his tone deadly serious. "I would never do that to you. If I'm doing something that appears dangerous—and you're involved—then I will tell you about it. I'll tell you beforehand. You'll know the score, like always."

# Chapter Eight

Jude got it right on our tenth, and final, set of foster parents. At the time, what I wasn't quite certain was why he even bothered. I mean, given what he was already capable of at that point, why bother with intermediaries? Why not simply cut out the middle-men, take what you wanted, and go tell the rest of the world to jump in the lake?

Perhaps it was that, by then, Jude had seen too many twisted, warped, manipulative foster parents who were utterly sanctimonious about their motives for wanting to "help" the poor orphan boys who were now in their teens. I don't know. It may just have been easier for Jude to set it up with a third party.

All I knew was that it freed us—again—from an institution that looked an awful lot like prison. We'd been in and out of so many rundown orphanages and state-run institutions by the time we were both seventeen that I was desperately willing to try anything to get out of the system once and for all.

We had one more year to go—one more year of high school as orphans and wards of the state. One more year of being shopped from foster home to orphanages for older boys like us who had no permanent set of parents, places that were really nothing more than slightly better-dressed prisons.

I had often wondered what would happen to us when we turned eighteen and were legal. I'd dreamed of the day often. Would they simply turn us loose from the system? Would we be allowed to go our merry way, thankful for the opportunity to be adults at last? Would they give us a stipend and a graduation certificate—"Congratulations.

You've survived family hell. Now it's time to go make your way in the real world as an adult"?

"I've found our adoptive parents," Jude said casually that August.

The last set of foster parents had turned us back over to the system at the end of the school year rather than keep us and the burden that went along with it. This particular set of foster parents had bought an RV with the ward-of-the-state money and were planning to visit Yellowstone and the Grand Canyon in it. They couldn't be burdened, of course, with two rambunctious teenage boys at the same time.

So we said good-bye to our third high school in three years and climbed into the dilapidated bus that took us fifteen miles down the road to Haverford Institution at the edge of Warrenton, Virginia. We were issued our standard ward-of-the-state uniforms, ushered into our ward-of-the-state rooms—complete with a toilet, sink, and bed—and were given instructions on when to show up for our three meals of the day and what we were expected to "contribute" to the upkeep of the place as our daily chores.

The only difference between Haverford and prison, in my mind, was that they didn't ask you to do chores in prison. In prison, you could just sit in your cell and read books, unlike Haverford, where fussy adult supervisors pestered you incessantly about things you had to do at various points of the day. I think I might have preferred prison to Haverford—but Jude took that decision out of my hands.

"Yeah, right," I said. "We go seventeen years without parents, and someone is going to adopt us now, right before the system turns us loose?"

"Better late than never," he said.

And then they showed up—a kindly, elderly couple from Charlottesville, Virginia, who'd never had any children of their own.

They'd driven up Highway 29 to Haverford to spend time with us. The next day, we'd climbed into the backseat of their car, and driven back to their farm on the outskirts of Charlottesville.

It was only later, after we were safely ensconced at our fourth and final high school as the newly adopted twin sons of this kind family, that I learned the truth.

The elderly man had once been a professor of theoretical physics at the University of Virginia. His wife of forty years had been a post doc under his care and guidance. Somewhere along the way, the physics professor had stumbled across an interesting way to permanently control and stabilize single layers of carbon atoms—graphene sheets—and then stack them one on top of another so they could form a variety of conductive materials that really big, multinational manufacturing companies could use.

The physics professor had carefully patented his invention and then sold the ideas to one big global company after another for royalties that would last nearly forever. He'd always been vague about the inspiration for his ideas. But it hardly mattered. He had the patents that clearly explained the knowledge, which meant he owned them.

Before long, the professor had become quite wealthy—beyond his wildest dreams, in fact—and was able to retire from his tenured faculty position at the University of Virginia. And ten years after that, the physics professor had seen his wealth accumulate into billions of dollars as the royalties from his patent literally poured into his bank accounts.

But that wasn't the truth. Oh, I'm sure this story played a hand in why Jude chose them as our final set of foster parents. But it wasn't the truth. It wasn't what really lived at the very center of this physics professor's life, what made him feel alive and consumed nearly every waking minute of every part of his day.

No, the truth was that the professor's marriage was a lie. He didn't love his wife, or even women for that matter. What he really liked, what made his heart race and flutter, were young boys.

Somehow Jude knew this. I didn't ask *how* he knew this. As in all things, Jude just knew it. He'd learned this man's secret and had chosen to take advantage of it.

Jude had, in some way, found a way into this man's life and heart remotely, which was common for these sorts of affairs. But Jude had deliberately sought him out rather than the other way around.

He'd cultivated the knowledge for more than a year without telling me. There had been text messages, then illicit photos, and then, finally, phone calls. By the time the elderly physics professor had learned he'd been played and conned, it was far too late.

The professor had no choice. Jude had him very carefully, tightly, and thoroughly wrapped up in a nice, neat package. And when Jude delivered the ultimatum—to accept us, both of us, into his little family, the incredibly wealthy former professor, who likely had thousands upon thousands of pictures stored away on his various computers, as well as electronic trails that would betray his true life's occupation, really had only one option.

The rules of engagement, in the end, were quite explicit and very clear. The man would leave us both alone—and Jude would, in turn, leave the elderly physics teacher to his own world and not reveal everything he knew to either the authorities or the business and financial world that had made him so very wealthy.

We took his last name, then, and became their adopted children. We would, at some point, inherit their vast wealth.

Knowledge is a curious thing. It holds a certain power. You can choose to do all sorts of things with that knowledge and with that power.

In the case of Professor Asher—who'd hungered for only one thing all his life, even as he'd amassed a fortune from a fortuitous discovery about the power of a single row of carbon atoms linked together—knowledge had never been a treasure stored up in his heart. It had been a burden.

But for Jude, once he'd unlocked this man's closely held secret and then threatened to shine a very bright light on it for the world, knowledge was indeed quite powerful. For Jude, it was a key that unlocked a door to a world that neither of us had ever truly known about—the world of privilege and wealth and freedom to go and do whatever we wanted without fear of being "sent back."

I must admit, I liked that freedom. I enjoyed it. I admired what Jude had done, even if I was simply not capable of the deed myself. I was glad he had found this guarded secret and had used it to give us a new life.

"It's all different now," Jude told me on our first day of school in our final year of high school. "We can do whatever we want. We will never have to do what others tell us, not ever again."

I looked over at him from the passenger seat of the brand-new Mercedes Benz convertible that he now owned and which was carrying us to our first day of class.

"And you think this will last?" I asked. "He'll just cut us out of his will the first chance he gets, you know. We can ride this for some time. But it won't last. It can't."

Jude smiled that smile. "Oh, I don't know. Once we turn eighteen, it won't matter as much. We'll have a legally binding trust. I've already arranged for that."

"A legal trust?"

"A legal trust, with no possibility of harm coming to it," he explained. "But there's more to it than that. I've also found ways to make myself useful to our new adoptive father in ways he'd never imagined."

"You don't mean that you …?"

Jude laughed mirthlessly. "Good grief, no, not that," he said, unable to keep the contempt from his voice. "He has no interest in *me*. Not now, not in that way. I'm far too old for him. I was able to keep my age a secret from him while we corresponded for those months. Once he found out how old I actually was, he recoiled. But it was too late. I knew everything that I needed to know about dear old dad-to-be by then.

"No, just as I'd deliberately sought him out, found him, and learned what truly interested him, so, too, can I help lead him to greener pastures than he's ever known or experienced," Jude continued. "There is a big, bold, awful world out there in the shadows and secret places, once you know where to look. I'm teaching him how to lift up heavy rocks and look behind closed doors that he's never even known existed. He has much to thank me for, actually."

I noticed then that Jude was gripping the steering wheel exceptionally hard. The blood had almost entirely drained from his fingers, which were wrapped around the expensive leather steering wheel of his new car. Jude may not have been able to articulate it, but I could see it.

He was angry—deeply, violently angry to his core. Jude knew what he was doing and was ruthless in his pursuit of what he wanted. But it didn't take away the anger at having to do this thing, to justify this particular end with these means in order to achieve financial freedom.

I almost said something at that moment. I'd *wanted* to say something to him, about how each of us, in our own way, had to do whatever we needed to do to survive and find our way in a world that didn't seem to care about our well-being.

I wanted to tell him that it was all right, that I was okay with what he was doing on our behalf, and that sometimes the end truly does justify the means.

I wanted to tell Jude that a person like Professor Asher never changed; that his own nature was so defined there was no turning back; that his own hidden life was one he'd chosen for himself and that it defined every single fiber of his being whether we liked it or not; and that we may as well profit from it.

But I didn't. Because, whether I admitted it or not, I thought that Jude was wrong, and I couldn't bring myself to think otherwise. I may have appreciated why Jude did what he did—and I may have been accepting of how that was now benefiting my own life—but I couldn't force myself to accept it. It seemed wrong, somehow, to profit from this man's carefully concealed secrets and pain.

"Don't get caught," I said instead. "Give me your word that you won't do something that's so out of bounds it follows us around like a black cloud."

"Oh, don't worry about that," Jude vowed. "We're never anywhere near the carnage. You can rest easy on that point."

It was then that I think I realized the awful decision Jude had made. In a world of suffering and pain that was not of his own choosing, my brother had decided to simply embrace the world as it was and to take from it everything that it had to offer in any way he so desired. He had not made the world he'd been born into—but he could certainly remake it as he saw fit.

# Chapter Nine

When I was healthy and physically recovered from my gunshot wound, I chose not to go back to work at the newspaper. At least not right away.

I gave up on the trip to the poor, warming Arctic Ocean that really should have been a harbinger to the world about what would happen to all of us within a generation or so if we continued to burn every last ounce of fossil fuels we extracted from the dark, deep corners of the planet. I would leave that story for another day when I was better able to tell it properly.

Someday, I vowed, I would more properly explain that unfettered, unrestricted corporate power built to unlock every source of energy on the planet would have unintended consequences for our human civilizations. I would do my best to explain what I'd learned from Jude over the years—namely, that human beings, if left unchecked, would take and take and take from the earth until they'd consumed everything within their grasp, leaving behind a husk devoid of value.

But not now. I needed to get my head clear of what had just happened. As much as I tried to understand it, the whole thing kept replaying in my mind with no suitable explanation. It made no sense.

Was it possible that Jude could have *not* known what was happening that day in the shadows of the new World Trade tower that had risen up majestically to replace the fallen Twin Towers? Was that truly possible, given what he'd learned from the regents and his fiancée? What was Jude not telling me?

I'd always assumed that Jude had controlled those largely unseen principalities and powers that he'd called on from a very early age.

After all, he'd managed to demonstrate quite a degree of control. From the very first moments when I'd watched Jude exert his own will through these unseen forces, I'd witnessed a certain level of mastery. They seemed to bend to his will without question. I'd never seen anything happen that Jude had not either foretold or planned.

Until the public square. I'd seen the anger, hate, and venom in that attacker's eyes. It had clearly been aimed in Jude's direction until I'd gotten in the way. But how was that possible? How? It made no sense—unless Jude was right that there were forces in that unseen world that he was still trying to understand and master.

I'd never read the Bible. I doubted I ever would. But I often heard stories that must have had their origins somewhere in the pages of that unusual collection that told of humankind's interaction with an all-knowing, omniscient God who ruled everything in His creation and loved each and every human unconditionally.

Stories about how you should love your enemies or treat others as you would yourself or feed the hungry and the poor—they'd almost certainly had their origins somewhere in the Bible. But I had no interest in searching out those stories or their meanings. I had Jude as my guide, from an entirely different vantage point.

Jude was quite clear about what the world meant. It was a place full of humans who were entirely self-obsessed. Each and every person struggled with daily existence, Jude believed, and strove to master small and great challenges alike on an entirely personal and self-centered basis.

Helping others was a luxury very few could afford. And those who did help others nearly always had plenty left over for themselves. Very, very few were utterly possessionless and willing to give all they had in both material and spiritual service to their brothers and sisters. That sort of selflessness, Jude believed, simply did not exist in the world.

For this reason, he always said, each and every human being on the planet was free to act in his or her own self-interest. Actually, it was more than that. Each one of us was *required* to act in our own self-interest, Jude believed, or risk being destroyed by others with stronger wills, more resources, and greater control of the natural environment. The strong survive. The weak fail. It really was as simple as that, Jude believed.

I had a difficult time disbelieving this worldview. In my own limited capacity, most people did go through their daily lives with blinders on that forced them to take actions and steps mostly benefitting themselves. Rules and laws kept people from veering into other's lanes, but I wasn't convinced that anything *outside* those physical rules and laws had much effect on people's mostly selfish actions.

Which was why I was so troubled by what had happened in the public square. It turned out that Samuel Chambers—the "policeman" who'd attacked Jude—was, in fact, a member of a group called the Christian Brigades, which now had unofficial chapters in several states in the American West. It was classified as an extremist hate group by domestic terrorism standards.

I wasn't all that troubled by the fact that there was a Christian Brigades. Such groups in America were hardly novel. From the John Birch Society on the far right to the Black Panthers on the far left, throughout history extremist groups had always grown at the edges of American society. Their fuel was hate, and their targets were those in authority. Groups like the Christian Brigades attracted people who believed that hate, bile, and venom were acceptable forms of human interaction.

You could nearly always see this in full display in the brave new world of instant media. Every story in every form of media always attracted commenters, and haters invariably came to dominate long comment threads. Expressing hatred toward those with whom we disagree seems to be a part of human existence.

No, what bothered me about the attack in the public square was that they'd selected Jude as the focus of their attack. Assassins targeted sitting presidents and elected officials, not mere candidates. It didn't make much sense to me—and, I knew, it perplexed my brother as well.

We both knew unseen forces were fully capable of channeling and directing hate and rage in certain directions. But this attacker, who had now been thoroughly debriefed by Homeland Security, had apparently acted on his own. His reasons for attacking were incoherent. He was clearly mentally unstable. He had no real motive, other than a likely objection to Jude as a member of the ruling order.

So it turned out Jude was no longer an innocent victim of an uncaring world. Now, at least to this particular person who'd chosen to sacrifice himself on the altar of violent infamy, Jude was a card-carrying member of the ruling order that controlled the lives of the lesser people of the earth. It was all very curious.

There was one person, however, who didn't seem to be bothered by all of this. In fact, Sandy was pleased by the unexpected turn of events. For, just as I was about to walk off the boyfriend cliff and burn yet another budding relationship with a member of the opposite sex, I'd suddenly come to my senses and stopped at the edge.

Sandy had come by to see me in the hospital after I'd been shot. She'd seen the horrific event on the news, of course, but had been unsure about whether I'd even want to see her again. When she'd walked through the entrance of my hospital room, I'd never been so glad to see another human being in my life—and I'd told her as much.

We went on our vacation together after all.

"So can we stay here forever?" I asked her the first day we were there.

Sandy lifted her head from the canvas deck chair she'd dragged out from the pool area at our Caribbean resort hotel. We'd planted ourselves right at the edge of the ocean, close enough to enjoy the gentle waves lapping against our feet, which dangled over the edges of the long chairs.

She squinted at me through the sun's welcoming, hot glare. "Seriously? You'd be okay with that? Just hang here, lying out in the sun, with no ambition beyond what we're going to have for dinner tonight?"

"My dear," I said casually, "I can think of nothing even remotely better than that right now. This is precisely what I'd like to do, and I would very much like for it to last as long as it possibly can. If I never return to work, I very well might be a happy man."

Sandy laughed. I could tell from the sound that it was real. She was genuinely happy with the turn of events in our lives. It might be some time before she'd trust me or my motives, but she was happy right now, at this moment. There was something to be said for that.

"You are such a silly man," she said. "Who knew that someone would need to shoot you in order to bring you to your senses?"

I grinned. "Oh, I'm not sure about bringing me to my senses. It's just that I never knew how delightful it could be to just do *nothing* for hours and hours on end. No cares, no worries, no meetings or phone calls to make, no people I'm forced to listen to or even care about. Who knew? I certainly didn't."

Sandy playfully nudged my toes. "It's called a vacation. Most people look forward to moments such as this, where they can relax and push the cares of the world off to the side for a bit."

"Well, I like it!" I declared. "So I vote that we stay here, just like this, for as long as we possibly can. I can have someone build a big cabana over us, right here on the beach. We'll have our meals delivered to us."

"And when you get bored? What then?"

"I won't," I vowed. "I have you to talk to. Conversation will carry us through each and every day."

"Sure." She chuckled. "That'll work. It will get us through one day, max. Then you'll find a convenient reason to wander off in search of a newspaper. You'll find a TV somewhere so you can catch up on what's happening in the world. Then you'll call your editor or one of your sources. You'll buy a laptop and start composing posts for the newspaper's blog pages. Then you'll—"

"Enough!" I threw my hands up toward the sky. "I get it. So this can't last forever. But can we at least enjoy this for a day? Right now? Can we commit ourselves to that? Can we promise that we'll allow this moment of doing nothing beyond merely existing on the surface of the planet to last for however long it's going to last? Can we do that?"

"We can, Thomas," she said gently. "And what's more, I will thoroughly enjoy every moment with you in that. It's all I've ever asked of you—and nothing more."

I didn't respond. I wasn't committing to Sandy beyond this pause in time. I couldn't. I didn't understand myself right now, much less another human being.

But I also knew I was happy she was at my side. I was happy to have a companion. Because, for now, the world seemed better with someone beside me who seemed capable of unconditional love.

# Chapter Ten

Jude and I, once inseparable, grew apart some in college. It wasn't deliberate on my part—it was mostly just geography and time. I just had better things to do, and so did he.

Most kids who arrive at college, parents in tow, full of hope and tears and joy at the promise of intellectual and physical freedom from the confines of family, very quickly fall into patterns and social cliques. Some join fraternities and sororities their first year if they're on campus. Others take up intramurals or hang out and talk about Plato's Cave until all hours of night in dorm commons or volunteer for various social causes.

I did none of those.

I was already free. I had no parents to speak of, beyond dear old Professor Asher and his hapless social companion. I was financially independent and truly had no real need to attend college to get a degree. I wasn't entirely sure why I was even bothering.

"Go to college. It'll kill time, and there's no reason not to," Jude had ordered somewhere around Christmas our last year in high school. "You're not Bill Gates, Steve Jobs, or Mark Zuckerberg—not yet, at least. You can always drop out of college when you'd like and pretend that you're like them."

That was typical of Jude. When all else failed, pretend to fall in line with social conventions and graces until a better idea came along. College was a logical next step for those with means and money—both of which we now possessed. So off to college we went.

Jude clearly had his eye on greater horizons, though he refused to talk about them in any specificity with me. Since Professor Asher had gone to Harvard as an undergraduate, we were now legacy kids. Not a sure thing, by any means, but Jude doubled on his bets by making Professor Asher donate to assure his spot at Harvard. He had his crimson wardrobe selected by the spring.

I went another direction. I had no real interest in college, a degree, or anything else for that matter. Honestly, I was a bit terrified at the prospect of living beyond Jude's shadow for the first time in my life. I didn't tell him that, of course. But it was literally freaking me out.

I figured it would be a bit weird and awkward to follow Jude to Harvard. I know that identical twins do that sort of thing all of their lives. They dress alike, hang out together, do all manner of things together, and quite often, make certain their lives intersect at every conceivable point. But Jude wanted to go out on his own, test his wings by himself. I could sense it. He wanted to fly toward the sun, and he didn't want a companion on that flight. I knew it. I could clearly see it. So I quietly applied to a few schools outside of the Ivy League and settled on Duke University in Durham, North Carolina, in the end.

Neither of us embraced or even said much beyond a quick good-bye when it was time to head off to college. That was fine with me. I wasn't sure how I would manage as it was, and the last thing in the world I wanted was for Jude to see me in my moment of weakness.

"See ya," I called out to him as he finished packing his Harvard wardrobe into the back of his convertible. "Call me every once in a while."

"No worries," he yelled back. "We'll see each other. Remember— everywhere is just a plane trip away."

We both laughed. Now that we had our own trust funds and a great deal of wealth at our disposal, that had become a running joke between us. We'd gone from wards of the state to jet-setters, thanks to a bit of surreptitious work and sacrifice on Jude's part. We were, in fact, never more than a plane ride away from each other or any destination on the planet. It seemed remarkably funny and surreal to us both.

I didn't bother to look back at the farm as I left in my own black BMW two-seater. Professor Asher wasn't on hand to see us off. I wasn't entirely sure where he was, to be honest. His wife said good-bye to us, at least, on our way out. I wondered if I would ever be back to that place.

Once I'd hit the open road, I flirted with the notion of just staying on I-81 as I drove south and west along the Appalachian Mountains, having decided to take a longer, more scenic route rather than the fastest. I didn't have to go to college. I could merely keep driving south, work my way around the country, and see whatever suited my fancy.

But I didn't. I dutifully followed the directions that led me out of southwest Virginia and into North Carolina. I arrived at Duke's campus that evening, unpacked my bags in the freshman dorm to which I'd been assigned, and prepared for the mind-numbing efforts to register for class, buy books, and get started with the next phase of my own education.

The one and only convenience I'd arranged was to pay extra for a single room in the freshman dorm. I had no desire or interest in a roommate. Jude had been my one and only roommate and companion my entire life—and I didn't want to face the prospect of trying to adjust to a stranger while I also adjusted to life without Jude.

It was a colossal effort to shift into the mind-set of college life. Who learns for the sake of obtaining knowledge? Who delays life for four years or more while they prepare intellectually for what they might do later in life? It was a bit jarring to me. Despite Jude's half-hearted order to me that it was the logical next step, I still had no use for it and wanted nothing to do with it.

Until I went to class. And then I got it. Suddenly, beautifully, almost magically, I understood. There was an entire other world out there that I'd never imagined. There was so little room for intellectual pursuit in America's public schools, which seem obsessively focused on making absolutely certain that the dumbest of us pass standardized tests.

College was precisely the opposite—it rewarded intellectual pursuit and philosophical passion. Any pursuit of any kind of knowledge was possible.

You could pretend that the world was illusion—that it was a mere figment of your collective consciousness—and you could find a philosophy class to reward such an intellectual journey.

If you were concerned about social injustice on other continents—or in America, for that matter—there were classes that grounded you in the basis of such injustice with historical, social science, and political teachings and writings.

And if you wanted to coast through college without thinking all that much about anything other than where the next frat party would be that weekend, you could do that as well. There were no intellectual limits.

I was beyond mesmerized. I could, in fact, see myself studying and reading and philosophizing in a college setting for years with no thought at all for what might come next. For the first time in my life, I was in love with learning. Granted, I could afford to drift. Unlike my peers at Duke, I would never worry beyond college about how to earn a living. Jude had taken care of that.

But that hardly diminished my ardor for learning. I was like a kid who'd been starved of sugar and who was now unexpectedly locked inside a candy store.

Largely because I couldn't settle on any one topic—and largely because there didn't seem to be any rules against it—I took on three different majors. I knew that I'd eventually have to settle on one of them for an actual degree, but that could wait. For the time being, I took classes in political science, international relations, and English as often as I could.

Jude and I talked frequently during our first three years of college. We visited each other. It was an easy trip from Raleigh-Durham airport to Logan in Boston, and we both made the trip several times a year. Neither of us went back to the farm for Christmas holidays. We took groups from college with us on skiing trips to Switzerland or safaris in Swaziland instead.

And we didn't return to the farm for the summer months either.

The summer between our third and fourth years, Jude went to New York for an internship with a brokerage firm on Wall Street. I joined him at an apartment in the city for an internship with NBC News at 30 Rock.

We were both about to turn twenty-one, which would be exciting because not only would it be legal to drink alcohol, but we'd be eligible for a much larger share of the trust than the spending money we'd been limited to as part of a legal guardianship.

It would be our last summer together, in one place.

Unbeknownst to me, Jude had already made plans for the next phase in his life. He called on his forces toward the end of that summer.

At first, I assumed he'd merely grown weary of living off his trust fund. He wanted access to more. Jude had never been one to wait patiently, and I figured he'd decided that he may as well cash in all his chips sooner rather than later.

Professor Asher and his wife contracted malaria while on a trip to sub-Saharan Africa. It happened suddenly. We'd heard, via email, that he'd gotten sick, and then his wife had as well, and that they'd both been flown to a hospital in South Africa for drug treatment. But they were much too far gone by that time. Their vital organs had already been compromised. Both were dead within the week. The bodies were flown home, and the memorial service was held in Charlottesville a few days later.

Jude didn't say much on the flight back to Virginia from JFK in New York. I didn't dare ask him whether he knew anything about what had happened.

But a casual comment made me think.

"He was starting to get religion," Jude said on that flight back for the funeral, "and beginning to feel sorry for all those kids over the years. He was muttering in his emails about giving it up and maybe coming clean. The trip to Africa was the first of many he was planning, part of an effort to set up a philanthropic foundation. He thought it might be a good idea to set up a foundation with his money before he died, so he could do some good. He was taking a serious look at how he could cut us out before we turned twenty-one. I couldn't have that. There was no way I could let that stand."

I didn't probe any further. I could imagine the way Jude had thought it out, though. If Professor Asher did, in fact, put his fortune into a foundation, Jude—and I, for that matter—would lose access to most of it. And it had to happen before we'd turned twenty-one and could make legal claims. While it made sense to me that a man such as Professor Asher would want to make amends at the end of his life and "do good" with his wealth, I could also see Jude's point of view.

But whether Jude could direct forces halfway around the world was another question entirely. But I didn't doubt his abilities to direct such forces.

After all, if human beings were only a plane trip away from any spot on the planet, then surely those who weren't bound by plane schedules could easily reach any spot on the earth as well, whenever they wished.

# Chapter Eleven

I made up my mind on the plane ride back from our Caribbean vacation. Sandy helped. She was delighted with my decision. I could actually see the smallest flicker of hope of a meaningful relationship.

"Oh, come on, you can't be serious," John Hargrove said, leaning forward in his desk chair. "A book? You're going to take a sabbatical to write a book? About what? Global warming? There are like fifty books on that subject, and a new one gets written about every other week. I mean, Bill McKibben's written about half of them, and they haven't convinced people yet."

The long-suffering science and environment editor at *The New York Times* was most likely jealous of my decision. I could afford to take a sabbatical, write whatever I felt like, and if an agent didn't like it or a publishing house didn't jump at it, I could just buy one of them and tell them to publish and market the book. I'd be jealous of that too.

"No, not global warming—though I *do* wish someone would write a real book about it someday that isn't built on predictions of likely future scenarios and computer-generated models about what might happen to the polar bears," I explained. "Some serious person should let the world know that the human species is in serious trouble because of our addiction to fossil-fuel-based energy. We're headed toward a tipping point of no return. Things will be quite bad in the relatively near future, with consequences that will cause a rapid transformation of what we now know as human civilization."

"But you won't be that serious person, I hope. Right?" Hargrove waggled a querulous brow.

"No, not me, I'm afraid." I laughed. "Not that I wouldn't mind giving it a try."

"So what's your book about then?"

I hesitated. I wasn't normally shy or reticent. But I also wasn't quite sure if Hargrove would understand why I wanted to pursue the topic of the book I had in mind. It might seem … strange to him.

"Well," I said slowly, "you know how there have been quite a few books on radical Islam fundamentalism since 9/11? Books on why and how people become jihadists, and why America has become a target?"

Hargrove narrowed his eyes. "You're not—"

I jumped back in. "No, not that subject. I don't know the first thing about Islam or jihadism. I would never consider taking that up. No, I'm only using that as a reference point. What I'm more interested in is why extremist hate groups have managed to rise in America and why we seem to have such an uncivil social dialogue in this country."

"So you want to take a look at the Christian Brigades." Hargrove frowned. "You're still upset that you were shot by one of them, aren't you?"

"No, no. It's not really that. But I don't completely understand what drives that sort of hate—or why it might be focused on someone like my brother."

"It's simple. They go after politicians all the time. People with that sort of crazy don't discriminate. If it gets them on CNN, that's the only motivation they need."

"Maybe," I said. "But Jude isn't elected yet. He isn't anything, really, other than a wealthy, famous person who's running for one of a hundred seats in the Senate."

"Who successfully bet against the Japanese yen and then the Chinese yuan, chaired the Federal Reserve, and is now one of the most widely regarded economic forecasters in the world," Hargrove added.

"Inside baseball, for Wall Street types and bankers. Not the public," I countered. "People of wealth and means know Jude—not the unwashed public. The public doesn't read *Forbes*. The keepers of the financial temple know all too well who Jude Asher is. But the people? They don't have a clue who he is, what he stands for, or why anyone would be motivated to hate him or even oppose him at this point."

Hargrove cocked his head. "So that's what you're curious about, then? You want to know why an extremist group like the Christian Brigades would take an interest in your brother and target him?"

"Among other things, yes."

"So, fine. Do that in your spare time. That's what the Internet is for—to search through hysteria and conspiracy-theory nonsense. I mean, good grief, just read through the thousands of awful comments on some of your own stories if you'd like to do some original research on hate speech."

"Yeah, I've had some doozies on a few of my stories," I said with a grin.

"So maybe that guy was really going after you—and not your brother," Hargrove half joked.

"Yeah, well, then he got his guy. My leg still hurts. The doctors said I'll probably have a permanent limp."

"I'm sorry about that." Hargrove's eagle eyes met mine again, this time even more intensely. "But I'm still waiting to hear why you need to take time off to write this book."

What I clearly could *not* tell him was that I wanted to write this book partly as a way to understand the forces that surrounded and served my brother—and which had somehow not managed to get in the way of an attacker when Jude had started to pursue public office. No, that wouldn't do at all.

"I just need to clear my head a bit, ask a few questions, and see what emerges," I said instead. "I want to do some research and see where it takes me, that's all. I need some time to do that."

"Can I at least get a few occasional dispatches from you from the field as you're wandering the nation on your quest?"

"Sure, why not? I can manage that once in a while."

"Good," Hargrove said. "So we won't lose you entirely."

"No, not entirely. Just for a time."

# Chapter Twelve

I was pretty sure I saw the first of them in human form at the memorial service. He was standing off to one side, respectful, polite, observant, and generally distant from the small handful of tenured and retired faculty members who came to pay their respects to Professor Asher and his wife in Charlottesville.

I can't tell you why, exactly, I felt with some certainty that he was one of them. Perhaps it was just that he didn't seem like he was there to pay his respects to the dead professor and his wife as they were lowered into the ground at a small cemetery behind a respectful mainstream Presbyterian Church at the edge of the small college town. He seemed like he was there as a courtesy—as if he were a dispassionate observer of the human condition at a moment of great sadness.

Funerals are not happy places. But, as is often the case, you can learn a great deal at times of crisis or despondency. In this instance, I noticed that Jude instantly took command of the situation. He greeted every person in the receiving line at the church and thanked them for their concern and prayers. He was unwavering in his willingness to stand there and express his depth of concern and care for his adoptive parents, who'd so graciously rescued him from the state.

And I kept an eye on Jude as he finally walked through the rows of crosses and headstones to greet the man who'd stood so patiently observing the service.

He was impeccably dressed. He'd clearly either come from money or inherited it. I assumed it was inherited wealth, not new money. He was far too comfortable with his regal bearing and attire to have come into it recently. The polite, observant, well-dressed young man looked as if he'd been well off for quite a long time. He was a bit too far away for me to see his features, but I could imagine he was quite handsome and imposing. That would make sense.

They talked for a few minutes. I could tell, just by Jude's body language, that my brother was paying very close attention to the conversation at hand.

When it was obvious Jude would be a bit longer, I drifted inside the church to get out of the heat. I wandered into the kitchen, found a can of Diet Coke in the refrigerator, and leaned against the sink. I enjoyed the way the cold, carbonated soda burned the back of my throat on the way down.

"He's a friend," Jude said, startling me.

I turned and faced my brother as he strode through the doorway that led from the church hallway to the kitchen. "A friend? You have those?"

Jude smiled. "Yes, I have friends now, at college. As do you, I believe."

"I very much doubt that the man you were speaking to is a friend from college. And why isn't he here with you now, in the kitchen?"

"He doesn't have much use for churches," Jude said casually.

"I see. So he's gone?"

"Yes, he had affairs to attend to and others to counsel."

"So he's an advisor?"

"Yes, among other things."

"Is he *your* advisor?" I asked, although I already knew the answer.

"Yes, I asked to meet with him. Now that we're entering a new phase, I wanted … more direct influence and discussion. I was tired of the guesswork."

"A new phase?"

"Our inheritance, Thomas," my brother said straightforwardly, as if explaining the obvious. "Once we turn twenty-one, we inherit the family fortune. We, you and I, will be quite wealthy. There are plans to be made, paths to be charted. We have a big transition in front of us now, with all that we're inheriting. We're no longer just college kids with trust funds."

"Oh, that. So he'll advise on that transition?"

"Among other things."

There was always so much I wanted to ask my brother. "So how should I think of him?" I asked instead. "As a … what? A trusted advisor to you on our affairs of state and inheritance?"

"Think of him like a regent. You know what that means, right?"

I rolled my eyes. "Yes, Jude. I'm the political science major, remember?"

"Good. So you know what he stands for."

"And will there be others like him?"

"There are many others like him, I would suspect."

"I meant around you—around us and our lives."

"They are always around us, Thomas, whether you wish it or not," my brother said. "But, yes, I daresay there will be other regents, other advisors from time to time. Our inheritance is rather large, you know—in the billions of dollars. Our dear departed dad's patents were awfully central to a great many companies and industries, it turns out. More than I'd first imagined. Sorting through them will be complicated and take some time and getting used to."

"So the need for your regent?"

"Yes, and the fact I wanted a certain directness in our relationship as we enter our next phase. It is a vast world now, with many opportunities before us." Jude's gaze appeared unfocused, far off. I could only guess what my brother was wondering about.

I broke into his thoughts. "So what will you do after you graduate from Harvard?"

He blinked. "Whatever I'd like, I suspect. But I'm in no particular hurry. I believe I'll just get my law degree from Stanford so I can see what the West Coast is like, and then I'll add my MBA on top of that. No reason not to finish off my college résumé. What about you?"

"I have no particular plans after college," I said truthfully.

"Well, find some. Because the world belongs to us now. Might as well take advantage of it."

# CHAPTER THIRTEEN

The survivalist retreat workshop was a good four-hour drive from the family farm in Charlottesville that Jude and I had maintained for years. We'd thought about putting the farm up for sale after our adoptive parents had died so suddenly, but Jude had quickly realized that it was, in fact, a great place to hold off-the-grid meetings with regents, moguls, or financiers that he didn't particularly care to be seen with in public.

The survivalist workshop had seemed like a good place to start on my research for the new book. There was a feeling of both impending doom and exhilarating liberation to simply walk away from the daily cares of the working world to explore whatever the day might bring. I had no idea what I was walking into, but I didn't care. For the first time in a long time, I was happy to simply exist with no plan or care for the future. I could almost see Sandy smiling somewhere at the notion.

I'd signed up for the retreat workshop on a whim after a skim through one of several wildly popular survival blogs. There were some tenuous connections—it wasn't like the Christian Brigades advertised for its recruits in handbooks that one could buy on Amazon—but I was fairly certain I'd trip across one or two potential candidates or actual members at such a retreat workshop.

Jude had simply laughed at me when I'd told him of my plans. "You're wasting your time," he'd said. "Those folks are all crazy."

"Maybe, but one of those crazy folks tried to kill you," I'd said while at his Senate campaign headquarters in midtown before heading to JFK for the flight down to Dulles. I'd decided to at least let Jude know of my plans.

"You do realize," he added, "that probably half of the people attending that retreat workshop you're going to are almost certainly informants or undercover agents from the FBI, ATF, DHS, or some other federal agency using it to spot troublemakers? Good luck trying to find anything real."

The Senate campaign was exploding with activity. The traditional bunting, in bright blue and white, flew everywhere. An enormous *Asher for Senate* sign was centrally located in the sprawling campaign office that took up an entire floor of the building we owned outright. Massive security ringed the office. Curiously, they were feds, not private security.

"I tried to keep them away," Jude told me. He'd built just one office for himself at the center of the campaign headquarters, with three open windows that faced out onto the floor, which was jammed with campaign workers. I felt a bit like a creature at a zoo in the office, but Jude didn't seem to mind. "I told the Homeland Security types that I didn't need the protection. An incident like that won't happen again. You and I both know that, but it's not like I can tell the federal authorities that."

"How can you be so sure it won't happen again?" I asked him.

"I'm sure," Jude replied. "It won't happen again. There's no good reason for you to go off hunting after those types either."

"It's something I want to do," I insisted.

"Whatever," Jude said dismissively. "But you're wasting your time, like all of this security around me here."

I peered out over the office. I could tell, right off, that none of the regents were there. The place bustled with activity, but none of the people appeared to be the kind I'd grown accustomed to seeing around Jude.

"It seems pretty chaotic," I said. "What are they all doing anyway?"

Jude shrugged. "Not sure, precisely. My campaign manager seems to have it well in hand. They have the ability to microtarget potential supporters down to the neighborhood and house now, so I'm sure they're identifying all of those types."

"And your unseen friends?"

"Not immediately here in this office," Jude said. "But don't worry. I'm safe. You go do your thing with your research, if you insist. But you're completely wasting your time. There's no actual rhyme or reason behind that phenomenon. It's built on fear of an uncertain future and not much else."

I deconstructed some of Jude's words as I drove along Highway 29 from the farm, the foothills of the Appalachians to either side of me. It was a peaceful, if uneventful, drive to the southwest of Virginia. Plenty of time to sort through priorities and questions that had been swirling since the shooting.

As I drove farther into the rural part of the state, I noticed that the towns got progressively less interesting as I made my way into the heart of coal country. Southwest Virginia was so far removed from the northern Virginia suburbs that I wondered how they were even remotely connected to the same state. No wonder that statewide candidates basically ran two separate campaigns—one for the northern Virginia suburbs, and a second for the parts of the state where workers clung to jobs in dying industries like coal and rural farming.

I was a bit depressed by the time I arrived in the county that housed the retreat workshop center. Not surprisingly, Google maps on my cell phone had been spectacularly unsuccessful at locating the lodge, which was deep in the heart of the woods off an old logging road. The Google car had not, apparently, bothered to make its way down these roads in coal country that existed somewhere between southwest Virginia and eastern Kentucky. I'd been forced to get out of my car at a rural gas station with pumps that still clicked and whirred when you filled the car with gas after it became apparent that my GPS wasn't cutting it.

"Yeah, you gotta turn behind the big, red barn with the chew tin on the side. Can't miss it. They just painted the barn," the gas-station attendant told me. "Take a left when you get to a fork, and then a right after that. You'll come out of a bunch of trees then, and it'll be up on top of the hill."

"Thanks much," I said. "I appreciate it."

The gas-station attendant gave me a curious look. "So you're one of those from the city who paid for the prepper stuff?"

"Prepper?"

"Yeah, you know, prep. Gettin' ready for disasters."

"Oh, well, yes," I said uneasily. "That's what I signed up for. It's a workshop."

He cocked his head to one side. "So what'd you spend on it? A few hundred bucks?"

"Yeah, something like that. Maybe five hundred dollars. I don't remember exactly."

The station attendant whistled. "Man, I'd love to get some of *that*, for sure. A good business, I'll bet, teachin' people how to prep for those backdoor nukes that North Korea's gonna drop on us one of these days, settin' all those welfare queens off against each other in the city once they can't live high off the hog no longer."

I studied the guy. He seemed to know an awful lot of the "prepper" language I'd seen sprinkled through some of the comment sections on survival blogs.

"You really believe that?" I asked him.

"What?"

"You know—about North Korea dropping a nuclear bomb on the United States and setting off a chain of disasters?"

The station attendant shrugged. "They got nukes, and they got missiles. They don't like America much, so, sure, I guess it's possible."

I wanted to tell the young gas-station attendant that, in fact, no, it wasn't possible. North Korea did, in fact, have nuclear weapons. So did Iran. But neither country was even remotely close to being able to mount a small warhead on an intercontinental ballistic missile capable of reaching the continental United States. There would be no "backdoor nukes" dropping on the US from Iran or North Korea anytime soon.

"North Korea doesn't like us much, do they?" I said instead.

"Nah, they don't." He glanced at my newest car, the latest in a long line of BMWs, which I'd grown accustomed to over the years. "So you got four-wheel on that car?"

"No, why?"

The attendant smiled. "Ah, just askin'. Good luck to you. Pray it don't rain while you're there, is all. You might need a tow for that thing if it does."

I returned the smile. "I'm sure I'll be fine. But thanks for letting me know."

"Anytime. Just bein' neighborly, is all."

As I drove away from the station, I wondered if, perhaps, the young gas-station attendant hadn't been playing with the big-city guy a bit. But he'd been right about a couple of things. It did seem silly, in retrospect, to drive to a survivalist workshop in a BMW. And, while five hundred dollars meant nothing to me and my deep checkbook, it did seem like those who *taught* about prepping—or retreating or whatever the survivalist language of the day was—were the true winners in this race to save humanity from disaster.

I found the big red barn. It *had* just been painted, and it would have been hard to miss. Curiously, the fading image of a tin of chewing tobacco had been left on the side, and the rest of the barn had been repainted around it. I wondered if they received advertising revenue for displaying the tin of chewing tobacco or whether the farmer just happened to like that particular brand and wanted the world to know.

The station attendant was right. As I wound along the old logging road, navigating my BMW up into the hills and around ruts on either side, it became increasingly clear that I would, indeed, be toast if it rained. There was no chance I'd make my way out of these hills. A four-wheel was a necessity back here.

His directions also had been spot on. The smallish wooden lodge was up at the top of a ridge, overlooking the valley. I wondered if the house had been specifically built for a purpose or if the owners merely liked the view.

I chuckled to myself as I parked my BMW on the grass three rows back from the other cars already gathered for the workshop. I spotted at least a half-dozen old Chevy Tahoes, another dozen or so F-150s and a smattering of Explorers, Jeeps, and Mountaineers. They were all four-wheels of one sort or another. Mine was the only exception.

I glanced at the license plates as I locked the car. Most were from Virginia, but quite a few hailed from neighboring states like North Carolina, Kentucky, and Tennessee. This wasn't a local gathering. These folks were genuinely interested in the concept of moving off the grid to a retreat.

"Now that's an awfully funny-lookin' BOV, if I've ever seen one," a voice boomed out to me as I walked between cars toward the front porch of the lodge.

I looked up at a rather large man with a faded, red-and-black plaid shirt, black jeans, and a raggedy baseball cap pushed halfway back on his balding head. He was leaning against the railing, watching me closely.

"A what? BOV?" I called back.

The guy moved around the railing to greet me as I came up the steps. He held out a welcoming hand. "You *are* new at this, I see. This your first workshop?"

I took his hand and nodded. "Yes, it is. I guess it's a bit obvious, isn't it?"

"Just a bit," said the man.

"So … BOV. What's that again?"

"Bug-out vehicle," the man said with a warm smile. "Generally an older four-wheel car with no fancy computer electronics that can get zapped by EMPs. And don't forget your BOB in the back."

I thought for a moment. "EMPs? Not sure what those are."

"Electromagnetic pulses. You know, when the Russians set off nukes in the upper atmosphere, knocking out all the electronics down below."

"I see." I did vaguely recall that the military had once been quite concerned about EMPs. It had never occurred to me that this same concept had managed to make its way into survivalist lore as well. "And the BOB? That would be … maybe a bug-out bag with the stuff you'll need as you make your getaway?"

"There you go!" he said, his voice unusually loud and clear in such a quiet place. "You'll get the hang of the prepper business in no time at all."

"Yeah, well, maybe," I muttered. "This is all pretty new to me."

"So what brings you out here in the middle of God's country, friend? And the name's Frank Gore, by the way. Or OTG Gore, as some of these folks like to call me."

"OTG?"

"Off the grid," he said. "It's the name of my blog and my handbook."

The light bulb went off. "You're teaching the workshop," I murmured. "Sorry. I didn't make the connection right away."

"No worries, friend. I'd hardly expect you to if you're not a regular reader of my blog." He folded his arms and waited.

It took me a moment to catch on. "Oh, sorry again," I said quickly. "My name is Thomas Asher. I'm from New York."

Frank Gore surveyed me closely. He didn't say anything right away. I could see that my name meant something to him. I couldn't tell if he was curious or repelled by the knowledge of who I was and where I'd come from.

"Yeah, I know who you are," he said finally. "But you're also from around these parts, up the road a bit in Charlottesville, if I remember correctly. You inherited that guy's estate?"

"The Ashers. Yeah, that's me," I said wearily. I'd long ago grown tired of trying to explain myself and my family history.

Gore tilted his head back a bit. "You're worth a lot of money, if I recall. What brings you out here to these parts, if I can ask? You're not exactly prepper material."

I decided to wade right in, though carefully. Sometimes, as a reporter, you had to make a calculated guess, an intuitive leap, to see if a source would play ball with you. If I guessed wrong, I'd blow up whatever chances I might have of extracting any meaningful information at this workshop. But if I guessed right, then I'd have a guide in this strange, new world I'd wandered into.

"I'm doing research for a book." I stared hard at Gore. "I'm a reporter for *The New York Times*, and I'm on sabbatical to write a book. I'm generally interested in the survivalist culture. So, no, I'm not exactly prepper material. But I'm awfully interested—and I'm hoping you can help me out and teach me the ropes."

Frank "Off the Grid" Gore started nodding, mostly to himself. I could see he was weighing his options. In the end, it appeared I'd guessed right. "I might be able to help out a bit," he said thoughtfully. "But we'd need some ground rules, of course. I have a reputation and a livelihood to protect."

"I can imagine," I offered. "I'm sure these workshops help the bottom line and pay some of the bills."

"You have no idea." Gore smiled. "It more than pays the bills, but that's a story for another day, perhaps. For now, I'd like to set the rules a bit. I'll help you out, show you the ropes, give you a bit of the history. In return, you leave me out of whatever you write. Sound like a deal?"

"Sure," I said. "But what do you get out of it?"

Gore chuckled. "Oh, you never know. I'm a friendly sort. And I like to talk. Maybe just leave it at that for the time being."

"Fine by me. So where do we start?"

Gore turned and led the way into the lodge. "You listen to my boring lecture, for starters. And we'll see how much of it you retain."

# CHAPTER FOURTEEN

The years immediately following the untimely demise—or fortuitous death, depending on one's perspective, I supposed—of our adoptive parents were some of the most productive of Jude's life. He was like a man who'd suddenly been released from prison. No excess was too much. No material thing was seemingly out of grasp. No woman, regardless of stature or celebrity, was out of reach.

I honestly didn't know how he managed to fit in as many clubs, red-carpet appearances, Broadway premieres, or celebrity sports-box events into his schedule. I mean, good grief, he was supposed to be going to law school at Stanford. But he traveled between both coasts constantly.

Even then, long before he actually became famous, Jude had started to appear on the arms of fairly well-known young actresses either already on the A-list in Hollywood and New York or about to be. Most of the photo captions simply referred to Jude as "wealthy, eligible bachelor" or something to that effect. The public, though, really had no idea who Jude was. Over time, that would change, but back then, his wealth, dark brown hair, green eyes, and lean-muscled physique were enough to attract stunningly beautiful young women. To Jude, it was a sport. He dated celebrities simply because he could.

At some point, he leased his own twelve-seat jet with two pilots on standby for spur-of-the-moment trips. Hardly what a law school student needed, but Jude wasn't your typical law-school student to begin with. By the time he'd finished law school and moved on to his MBA back at Harvard, he had the whole go-to-school-and-jet-around-the-globe thing down to an art. He could seemingly be in three places at once and not miss a beat.

He included me on some of the trips, when I could either afford the time off or just felt like a long weekend. I didn't have to work. But I *wanted* to do something productive, and I had no interest in the family business—whatever that actually was. Jude could manage the many companies that profited from with Professor Asher's graphene metamaterial patents.

I knew Jude and his coterie of regents were rapidly expanding the family business, if only because my own accounts grew exponentially. At some point in those years after college, I simply stopped paying attention to the various bank accounts. I had enough money to do anything I wanted, anywhere, at any time. I could buy a house in every country of the world and pay cash. I could travel 365 days a year and stay in the best hotels on the planet, and it wouldn't make a dent in my bank accounts.

But I had no interest in those sorts of things. I couldn't say exactly what I wanted to do, but I knew aimless travel wasn't it. So I took a job with *The Herald-Sun* in Durham after my years at Duke and became a reporter covering local and state politics. I didn't mention to anyone at the paper about my inherited wealth and, quite curiously, hardly anyone asked me about it. Apparently few in Durham, North Carolina, were able to make the connection between the always-unnamed Jude Asher who regularly appeared in *People* and *US Weekly* and the guy who looked like him and worked as a reporter at a dying newspaper in a town built with tobacco money.

"Wouldn't it be easier if you bought the paper?" Jude had once asked me. "For that matter, just buy one of the newspaper chains or a couple of the national magazines and make yourself publisher."

"What would be the fun in that?" I'd shot back. "Where would the challenge be if I merely bought my way in?"

I wondered, every so often, if Jude had a goal in mind with his vastly accelerating wealth. Most likely. But, curiously, Jude had not succumbed to that old adage about the love of money being the root of all evil. Actually, Jude had very little use for money, and he certainly neither lusted after it nor loved it any demonstrative way.

No, he simply saw money and wealth—even vast, insane, mind-blowing wealth—as little more than a path. To what, I couldn't say. But I was certain Jude paid only as much attention to the accumulation of wealth as was absolutely necessary. He left most of those details to his regents.

The regents, by the way, had very little to say to me. They tolerated me in a cold, unapproachable way. It was Jude they served slavishly. In those first few years after college, more of them showed up every time I journeyed with Jude somewhere, seemingly spawned and cloned from a place where finely tailored suits, polished leather shoes, and manly perfumes were freely available.

My first face-to-face encounter with one of them was strange. We were in Las Vegas for a world heavyweight title fight. Jude had sent the jet to fly me in for the fight that Saturday evening after I'd complained that I had a deadline to meet and couldn't take a commercial flight out to Vegas at the last minute. The jet had waited at Raleigh-Durham airport for me while I'd finished writing my story and filed it.

But, before the fight, Jude had warned me, we were all going to a standup comedy show with Jerry Seinfeld at the MGM Grand that was almost certain to attract paparazzi. Seinfeld only did a few shows in Vegas, and the stars came out in droves when he did. Jude had lined up dates that evening—for both of us—with two actresses even I'd heard of who both had movies in theaters nationwide.

When Jude picked me up from the jet on the tarmac, a regent was with him. It wasn't the same one I'd seen at the memorial service, but it may as well have been. I could barely tell the difference. He had that same distant, cold, unapproachable look. He shook my hand firmly, introduced himself to me as Jude's business associate, and then turned his attention back to Jude almost immediately. They were discussing one of the companies in the portfolio of businesses he was clearly managing for Jude—and me, to a lesser extent—when we picked up the two actresses for the evening.

That's when I first noticed it. I had to admit, it unnerved me a little. A group of photographers were smoking cigarettes and casually hanging out in front of the hotel as we pulled up in front with the limo. The regent hung back as Jude and I got out of the car. He let the photographers snap their pictures of us and emerged from the car only after the paparazzi scattered like mice when they'd realized no one famous would be emerging from the limo. The regent then walked by Jude's side toward the hotel entrance.

Then, as the two actresses left the hotel, one after the other, I caught the regent moving effortlessly off to one side, flanking the paparazzi. He was behind the photographers as they snapped away madly. Now curious, I kept glancing at the regent as we walked from the hotel entrance back to the limo. He never appeared in a single shot the paparazzi took. I was fairly certain of it. The regent even waited until all four of us were safely inside the limo and the paparazzi had begun to tuck their cameras into their bags before rejoining us.

It was the same drill at the MGM Grand. Even more paparazzi were there, staking out the entrances as each star made his or her way inside for the Seinfeld show. The regent held back, vanished briefly off to one side, and then reappeared with us once we were safely inside and headed to our front-row seats. The regent sat apart from us, two rows up and well clear of even wide-angle photo shots.

And, after the show, as we made our way to the fight, the same sequence happened all over again. The regent was never in a single picture. By the end of the evening, I knew the regent was either extraordinarily camera shy, or he had a good reason to make sure he was never in the same shot as Jude. I couldn't tell which.

Later that evening, more out of idle curiosity than anything else, I typed my brother's name into Google Image search and scanned through hundreds of pictures. There were lots of them already, mostly because of the celebrities he was accompanying. But, as I'd suspected, there wasn't a single picture of a regent in any of them.

It was as if the regents—those who surrounded my brother, at least—didn't exist, at least not in a way that seemed entirely logical to me.

# CHAPTER FIFTEEN

Frank Gore was certainly right about one thing. His lecture was boring. But it hardly mattered to me. It wasn't like I was planning to go out and load up my BOV and pack up my BOB anytime soon.

But the flow of language from the audience members sitting and listening in rapt attention *was* interesting. Clearly, everyone here—with the possible exception of Frank and me—was waiting for one apocalypse or another to rain fire and brimstone on America and cause panic, mayhem, and violence to sweep through major urban cities.

Frank's opening talk focused on the basic facts that everyone needed to pay close attention to when looking for a retreat location as far off the grid as possible. A source of fresh water, of course, was essential. A spring would be ideal, but a well could work. Arable land so they could grow their own food once the stockpiles ran out was important. So was southern exposure for natural warmth and so the solar panels, needed to convert the sun's radiation to electricity—photovoltaics—that they would bring along to satisfy their energy needs would get sun exposure.

There were other things I'd never even considered—like looking for someplace that wasn't prone to flooding, tornados, or other natural disasters. And naturally, you wanted to steer clear of nuclear power plants and areas that real-estate developers might someday consider valuable pieces of property.

But the one that got me was the choice about whether to build one's basic retreat on a hilltop with open fields below that constituted "defensible terrain," or whether to hide the house away from the line of sight of any major road or highway.

"Guns or Gone," is the way Frank put it. Either opt for the concept of holding the high ground with firearms and a field of fire clearly outlined below in case attackers stormed the retreat on the hilltop—that was the "Guns" part—or carefully conceal the retreat behind lines of trees well away from any line of sight from roads so no one could ever find it. That was the "Gone" part.

"Above all, get out West, in my opinion," Frank concluded. "The East Coast will be choked by everyone fleeing from the big cities like New York where the folks who've been on the dole all their lives suddenly have to run when disaster strikes. Go find yourself someplace that has both farming and timber potential. Don't go anywhere near the coasts. Too much risk of hurricanes and storm surge. And, by all means, stay as far away from the Mexican border as you can in case the civil war there sends even greater stream of illegals across the border."

I didn't think Frank was a racist. His occasional cracks about welfare queens and illegals were used to elicit knowing smiles and nodding. I figured he mostly just knew his customers. They were all blue-collar, middle-aged white folks who seemed to genuinely believe that all hell was about to break loose in America—either when the president declared martial law, China sent a deadly version of the bird flu across our borders, or God turned the bowls loose and sounded the various trumpets.

I couldn't tell whether any of the retreaters, or preppers, had a particular disaster scenario at the ready. They mostly just felt a general uneasiness about the state of things in America and wanted to get as far away from big cities, bright lights, and the centers of civilization in the country as they could. And Frank was there to help them do just that, either through his workshop, his handbook, or his survival blog.

Honestly, I came to admire Frank by the end of the lecture and question-and-answer period. I couldn't help it. I had a soft spot for true entrepreneurs, and Frank Gore had certainly found his niche. I wondered how much of what he talked about was actually what he believed—and how much was window dressing. Most likely a bit of each.

I also admired the way in which Frank took every question in stride, no matter the spin or direction.

"Can we grow our food without chemicals, please, or will we need to worry about fallout that might contaminate our food?" asked a woman who wore no bra; had her hair piled up and held together with not one but four wooden sticks; wore a lengthy, hand-stitched, all-cotton dress that dragged along the ground as she walked; and wore actual Birkenstocks.

This particular style of prepper, I later learned from Frank, was a relatively new style of retreater. More and more, he said, folks coming from the hard left and eco movements, who were genuinely worried about looming ecological disasters, were showing up at retreat workshops or paying for his monthly blog newsletter. They seemed interested in getting back to nature, much like those who had created communes a generation earlier.

"Well," Frank answered slowly, "it all depends on where you are. If you're well away from a nuclear power plant and major urban centers, then there's much less chance of fallout or chemical contamination. That's why I like the western part of the country—you can grow your food naturally and don't have to worry about contamination of any sort."

The woman, delighted, beamed at the answer.

"So should we stockpile as much generic ammunition as we can, in case we need to go to a straight barter system when cash becomes worthless, or are straight boxes of gold coins better?" asked a man. He looked like the type who had likely once purchased everything he could afford from the Harley-Davidson catalogue and rode around the countryside on the weekends. But now he had opted for a double-stitched wool shirt, a down jacket, all-weather boots, aviator sunglasses, and durable blue jeans that could accommodate both a handgun and a Buck knife.

"Excellent question, sir. Very perceptive." Frank pointed knowingly in the questioner's direction. "Truth is, you're likely better off with the extra boxes of ammunition. Gold is fine, of course, but you might have to find someone who will accept it. Ammunition can either be used or traded for other goods you might need right on the spot. So I'd go with the stockpiles of extra ammunition."

I almost raised my hand. I wanted to ask Frank, publicly, if any of this was really necessary; if maybe we weren't all a little unsettled by an economic recession that threatened all sorts of blue-collar industries and jobs; if, perhaps, we weren't simply fantasizing about a gentle, easygoing far-off place where incessant bills that had to be paid didn't arrive in the mail each day and where we didn't have to worry about getting mugged, robbed, beaten, or raped when we ventured out late at night in any number of big cities in America.

But I didn't, of course, because that would have blown Frank's cover. And, from what I could tell as I'd watched the workshop progress, Frank was the sane one who could provide a road map that might lead me to groups like the Christian Brigades burrowed deeply in the shadows of America's new off-the-grid subcultures.

I waited patiently after the workshop ended as one well-wisher, truth-seeker, or hero-worshiper after another had a private word with Frank. Nearly every one of them had brought their cherished handbook—*Off the Grid*, by Frank Gore—with them. Most asked him to sign it. Frank's signature work was, apparently, an extraordinarily popular piece of literature. No wonder he'd referred to himself as OTG when we'd met.

"That was quite a show," I said when only the two of us were left in the lodge.

"Yeah, I aim to please," Frank replied.

"What's the old saying? 'Always give them their money's worth'?"

"Amen to that, brother." He laughed.

I scanned the lodge and added up the number of chairs. There had been close to one hundred people here this evening. Frank watched me closely, trying to gauge my intentions. "So for a gig like this …?" I said.

"I clear about four grand for an evening workshop," Frank said quickly and directly. "Hardly any overhead, and the marketing takes care of itself with my blog and newsletter and word of mouth. I assumed that was what you were about to ask?"

"Yeah, it was. Not that it's any of my business. I mean, people pay money for all kinds of things."

"So why not to learn how to survive the coming apocalypses?"

"Pretty much. It's nice work, if you can get it."

Frank got up from his chair with effort and eased toward the front porch. "Arthritis," he explained as he walked along. "I'm up to a triple dose of ibuprofen a day. Doesn't help much."

"I'm sorry."

"Not your problem, and there are plenty of other ailments that could be worse. All in all, if this is the only chronic pain I have to deal with, I'm fine with that."

The last of the cars were pulling away as we reached the porch. I could barely make out the red taillights as they winked through the trees at the edge of the clearing.

"So what is this place anyway?" I asked.

Frank laughed. "Used to be a KKK lodge."

I glanced at him. He seemed to be serious. "Really?"

"Yeah, really. The KKK is long gone from these parts, though. I've used it a bunch of times over the years. It's a great place for these workshops. Centrally located in this part of the country. Folks can drive here from Virginia, North Carolina, Tennessee, and Kentucky."

I nodded. "I know. I spotted license plates from all those states when I pulled in."

Frank slowly and deliberately cracked the arthritic knuckles on the fingers of both hands, then rolled his head from side to side in an effort to ease some of the pain he was clearly experiencing in his neck from the evening of lecturing. "So you gonna tell me why you're *really* here, Thomas Asher? 'Cause it sure as shootin' isn't about the survivalist subculture or preppers or retreaters, is it?"

"No, Mr. Gore, it isn't," I said honestly, deciding that I needed to take the risk and see how far I could get.

"So what, then?" he said easily. "You figurin' that maybe I know something about that guy who shot you in New York, maybe? That have something to do with it? You're tryin' to do your homework on that group, the Christian Brigades, and the connections they might have to some of the folks who sign up for my newsletter and handbook? Do I have that about right?"

I stared back at him, impressed. "You're a smart man, Frank Gore. You aren't all that you seem at first glance."

"My momma didn't raise no fool, as they say," Frank said lightly.

"And if I had a momma, that might be true of me as well," I replied. "Now, about the Christian Brigades. Can you help me?"

"I might be able to, Mr. Asher. I just might. But you should be prepared for what you might find. They can be a bit like the Knights Templar order centuries ago. They're out to protect someone or something for reasons that don't always make sense. Catching hold of them is like chasing a cloud. They always seem to retreat into the mist."

# Chapter Sixteen

"It's not like some bet in Vegas," I warned my brother on our twenty-fifth birthday. "You're talking about a huge gamble, with a whole lot of the money we've inherited."

"It's not a gamble," Jude insisted. "I know what I'm doing. More importantly, the regents know *precisely* what they're doing."

I'd looked around the deck of the cruise ship that Jude had rented out for our birthday celebration. It was comical. Jude had rented an entire cruise ship for three days—the whole thing, every berth—to celebrate in style. He'd invited hundreds of our "closest friends" for the party. I knew, at most, twenty or so of them.

Standup comics and top-tier rock bands were performing. There was a world-premiere launch of a new Hollywood film. He'd even managed to convince the cast and crew of the most popular reality television show in America to film an episode aboard the ship during the party. Jude had spared no expense.

"By the way," I said to him, as we viewed the festivities from the captain's quarters high above the ship's deck, "was this absolutely necessary?"

"Go big or go home," Jude said with that megawatt smile of his that was rapidly becoming a trademark. "It's all illusion, brother of mine. Just a big show."

"And you're the center of attention."

Jude shrugged. "Someone has to be. Might as well be me. It could be you as well, if you'd ever loosen up and enjoy what we have."

There was no need to answer him. Jude knew where I stood. We'd had this argument so many times that neither of us even brought it up much anymore. Jude wasn't about to change the way he grabbed the world by the throat, and I wasn't about to change my own habits anytime soon either.

"So this bet?"

"Not a bet," Jude said. "I've been studying it for six months now. My advisors assure me that it's all headed in this direction."

"You mean your regents," I corrected him.

"Whatever."

"Speaking of which …"

"They're around. You know, one of these days, you'll stop asking that question."

"All right, all right," I grumbled. "So your *advisors* tell you that this thing makes sense. Why?"

"Because they know what's happening at the nation-state level. The new Japanese prime minister is serious about finally devaluing the yen. He desperately needs to boost their exports to shore up their economy."

"You're talking about that principalities and powers stuff?"

"Yeah, that," Jude said casually. "They're never wrong about those things. When they say a world leader or a government is going to do something, go a certain direction, it happens. And, in this case, it means that the yen is going to be devalued. We're going to gamble on that, bet against the yen."

There was a sudden burst of activity below. Glancing down at the deck, I watched as deckhands started to clear the center of the ship and bring in barrels and boxes. "Something else you've cooked up?"

"Fireworks—to celebrate our own independence day four years ago," Jude said.

"Like they're gonna get that."

"Like I care. The fireworks are for me—and you. Our own private joke."

"Great," I mumbled. "So, seriously, Jude, tell me—how do you *know* this will happen with the yen? Japan's leaders have been trying to devalue the yen for twenty years without any success. People have tried to short Japan for most of that time. I think they call it a 'widow maker' on Wall Street. What makes this time any different?"

Jude turned away from the festivities below to face me, as if he wanted to make certain that I understood. "Because this time *I'm* asking the question and demanding the right answer. I studied the situation with Japan's leadership and national intentions and asked the regents to tell me what would happen. I'm satisfied with the answer. It's that simple."

Weirdly, I believed him. When it came to Jude, he'd never failed to get what he'd wanted or sought. Not really. This was a much bigger lift, with more at stake. But, in the end, it did seem to be that simple. Jude was asking the question, and he was almost certain to get the answer he wanted.

"I get it." I nodded. "So how much are you putting in play?"

"A good part of the $15 billion in the hedge fund," Jude said. "I figure we'll make almost $2 billion if the yen falls the way I know it will."

"What do you need to make that bet?"

"The dollar buys about eighty yen right now," he explained. "I need it to buy more than one hundred yen to the dollar over time. If it does, we'll make $2 billion on paper."

"And if the yen doesn't fall? If it goes the other way?"

"Then we'd lose that much," he said in a straightforward tone. "But trust me, it won't."

"And are you, or we, telling anyone about this gamble? Not that I care one way or another. Just curious."

Jude remained calm, unruffled. "No, we're not. This is merely a test, mostly on my part. I want to see how some of these reverse-knockout options work. I don't need this to be public—not this time."

Six months later, almost to the day, *The Wall Street Journal* reported that Germany and France intended to take legal action against Japanese government for its successful efforts to devalue its own currency, boosting its trade and exports.

Other countries—those as dependent on exports as Japan—quickly announced that they would join the efforts of Germany and France and take action to reduce their own currencies in order to remain competitive with Japan.

There was a flurry of activity at every level on the world economy. Investors and hedge funds changed their ratios on the yen. Financial analysts predicted that Japan's six-month antideflation efforts would rapidly come to an end.

The dollar brought in 105 yen on that day, up from eighty yen six months earlier. Jude, on the advice of his regents, pulled back all of the efforts to short Japan on that day. But not before we'd made nearly $2 billion in six months, just as Jude had predicted.

# CHAPTER SEVENTEEN

I'd have been lost without Frank Gore's road map, frankly.

As Jude's Senate campaign progressed throughout the late summer and fall months that led to the general election, I crisscrossed the country by myself to call on various places Frank recommended I casually, unobtrusively visit.

Meanwhile, my own newspaper and others now predicted an easy, twenty-point landslide win on the basis of a combination of Jude's name recognition, financing, leadership network, and activist groups that fanned out across the state to literally go door-to-door to round up every conceivable "issue" voter who'd ever identified with progressive issues—from gun control and immigration reform to climate change and marriage equality.

As for me, I tucked Jude's Senate campaign into the far recesses of my mind. I knew what he hoped to get from the Senate, and I was equally certain he would win the Senate seat as a first step toward a larger political objective. Jude had always gotten what he wanted, and politics would be no different. Unless there was an intervention or a mistake out of his direct control, he would become president.

On Frank's gracious recommendation and invitation, I didn't visit these places as a reporter for the *Times*. I wasn't shy about who I was when pressed, but I didn't lead with that.

Instead, Frank agreed to be a researcher for my book project. That, in turn, allowed me to simply tell people that I was working with the great "Off the Grid" Frank Gore on a new project. The mention of Frank's name was like magic—better than anything I'd ever seen in my life.

It was extraordinary. Clouds of suspicion on people's faces simply vanished when I mentioned I was working with Frank. They broke into knowing, welcoming smiles of recognition. We were, almost instantly, fellow travelers with a common language and an unspoken calling and mission.

I was also frankly shocked at what I found in the remote parts of the United States, especially out West in place like the Dakotas, Idaho, and Montana. People were serious about their homesteading. They'd adopted every word from Frank's handbook and blog as if the words had come straight from God's mind and a burning bush.

I was welcomed into homes by people who, honestly, should have known better. But if I was Frank Gore's friend and I was working with him, then I was welcome almost anywhere.

I very quickly learned the secret words and phrases that unlocked any manner of new lines of discussion about fears of a centralized government; worries that America had lost its moral center; a belief that poor, single mothers would rather live in Section 8 housing in big cities and have lots of kids than work; an uneasy sense that any number of disaster scenarios were just over the horizon; or thoughts about how huge, global corporations were soulless, greedy, ravenous entities that served only themselves.

More importantly, I learned an even better secret—the art of asking questions and then shutting up. Most reporters take years to actually learn this secret. But it was invaluable here. I could simply keep asking questions, and people opened up.

Because I'd arrived with Frank Gore's blessing and I wasn't talking about my own beliefs or views—I was simply listening to theirs—I was able to spend countless hours, days, and weeks soaking up the heart of a subculture I'd never even known existed in America.

One thing became abundantly clear to me: whatever the big power centers in New York, Washington, and Los Angeles believed they knew about the other parts of America, they were simply wrong. There was another America that didn't believe a single word that was written, spoken, or displayed from any institution associated with or established in these centers of American culture, politics, or finance. Not a single word.

This—among all the aspects of this other America I was learning about—is what shocked me the most. Oh, people were polite about it. They talked in calm, easy, almost-casual tones about the political, financial, or entertainment worlds.

But deeper, below the surface—as I was now, thanks in no small part to Frank Gore's social-network connections—I very quickly learned the truth. These people held deeply entrenched, foundational beliefs that weren't reflected in the media or political discussions. Vast parts of America not only distrusted their leaders, they reviled them. They believed—with passion and conviction—that corporate, political, and financial leaders were liars, thieves, crooks, and moral reprobates.

They took every word they heard from these leaders and assumed the opposite was true. They took every action and assumed the worst intentions. This other America was utterly, unequivocally convinced of the self-centered, greedy, and even immoral aims of the leaders of industry, finance, politics, and entertainment. And there didn't appear to be anything that would move them or convince them otherwise. They'd moved as far away from the power centers as they possibly could, and there seemed to be no going back.

Hints about the mysterious Christian Brigades wound their way through several of these conversations. But they were always just that—hints. The group wasn't physically located anywhere. People knew of them or had heard of them. Their adherents, like the Knights Templar, seemed committed to a larger crusade. But whenever I found myself getting closer to some sort of truth about the Christian Brigades, the information drifted off into the mist. I nearly gave up my pursuit of them.

In fact, I often wondered, late at night, as I collapsed in my hotel room, whether I'd wandered down into some abyss I would never be able to forget. How could a people, even a subculture, genuinely structure their lives and families around hopelessness, fear, mistrust, and even hatred? How could you believe that your lives and your communities meant something when you also believed that everyone else in every other part of the world was out to harm you in some fashion with their words or actions? How could escaping "off the grid" be something of value to anyone beyond yourself and your immediate family?

But then a curious thing happened. I headed to the city that I'd heard had, without any thought or planning, become the de facto, unclaimed capital of this new confederacy of disenchanted, disaffected, mistrusting, and perpetually angry mob who genuinely believed that "off the grid" was their salvation and path to freedom.

I came to Bozeman, Montana. And everything changed.

# CHAPTER EIGHTEEN

Jude was in his midtwenties when fame began to follow his fortune.

"Why that one?"

It had been a logical question that day in Kentucky, when Jude was still trying to build his brand and name recognition beyond financial circles. But that wasn't what I had been asking Jude, and he knew it. So he waited for the handlers around us to provide their answer. And then he told me the truth.

That day had been preceded by a trip two years prior to the yearling sales at Keeneland's racetrack. There we'd spent the days prior to the yearling sales wandering around the various barns and listening to young sheikhs from Saudi Arabia ask questions of the trainers and owners about the young horses that would shortly go up for bid.

Jude had known very little about bloodlines, famous or otherwise, prior to that Keeneland auction. But he'd learned a great deal in a very short period of time, and he settled on a young bay colt from an undistinctive sire for reasons I hadn't asked about at the time. He'd paid $2 million for the yearling, based on advice from the various handlers, trainers, and racehorse bloodline experts who'd flown out to the sales with us to advise Jude on his purchase.

But I'd known that Jude wasn't paying much attention to those various handlers as they gave him advice on which yearling colt to purchase—other than to make certain that the horse he eventually *did* buy at the auction had at least some modicum of respectability in the racing world and wouldn't seem outrageously overpriced when he bought him. Jude had a plan for this horse.

"Because it will make a truly incredible story when he wins," Jude told me as we strolled through the grounds of Churchill Downs on the day of the Kentucky Derby.

"What makes it a great story?" I asked him, more out of politeness than conviction. I didn't even bother to ask why he was so convinced that the horse he'd purchased two years earlier would win. If Jude said his horse would win, it would win.

"When was the last time a horse won the Triple Crown?" Jude asked.

I'd never been to a racetrack before, much less a track like Churchill Downs during the Kentucky Derby. It was quite a spectacle. Extraordinarily wealthy, older women in broad hats and pearls walked side by side with regular bettors who came to the track every day to scratch out a living or lose their last paycheck. Men in tailored suits who would never ordinarily set foot in a place that reeked of urine and stale beer chose to stand with the rest of the rabble to watch the horses on parade before taking their spots at post in the first leg of the Triple Crown. I was thoroughly enjoying myself. It was the kind of place where a fortune could be won or lost by anyone with any means.

But Jude wasn't here for those reasons, and I knew it. "I really don't know all that much about the Triple Crown," I said, "so I couldn't even begin to tell you who won it last."

"At all?"

"No, not at all," I confessed. "I'm assuming there are three races?"

Jude laughed at my naïveté. "Yes, three races. The Kentucky Derby is the first leg. The second leg is in two weeks. It's called the Preakness, in Baltimore. The third and final leg of the Triple Crown is the Belmont in New York. We're going to be in Baltimore, and then New York for the last leg—cheering on our horse as it attempts to win the Triple Crown. Three-year-old horses that win all three races are considered the greatest horses of all time and take their place alongside horses like Secretariat."

I shrugged. "Okay, so it's a few horse races. What's the big deal?"

"The big deal," Jude answered, "is that millions and millions of people pay attention to the Triple Crown every year. They may not pay attention to horses at any other time, but they do when it's the Triple Crown. They learn all about the horses, their trainers, and their owners. Every racehorse owner who has ever lived has hoped to see their horse in the Kentucky Derby someday. The Kentucky Derby is like the Super Bowl or World Series of horse racing. The best of the best compete here, and only the very greatest are capable of winning all three races in a row. The last time a horse won the Triple Crown was in 1978, a horse named Affirmed. It's been decades since Affirmed, and the world pays attention every year to see if a new champion will emerge."

"But one hasn't since 1978?" I scratched my head. "So you paid $2 million for that yearling two years ago hoping it would be good enough to compete here and pursue the Triple Crown?"

"Yes, we did," Jude said. "But not just any old yearling. I wanted one that had two important aspects. I heard all the experts about the horses' bloodlines, and then I asked the regents to identify the exact type of horse I was looking for. They found that yearling, and that's the horse we bought."

"Which was?"

"A yearling that had a compelling story behind it, that would capture the public's imagination if it won. But it also had to have bloodlines that would make sense to the racing world as well—a horse that could withstand the grueling nature of the Triple Crown. It's why part of his bloodline includes probably the most correct broodmare sire in history, Buckpasser. But that isn't the real story behind our horse."

I looked out over the parade of horses walking along with their handlers, trying to find the colors Jude had selected for Asher Racing. I found the black, red, and gold through the throng of people and gazed at the magnificent bay colt as it seemed to dance lightly alongside its walker.

"So what *is* the story behind the horse you bought?" I asked him.

"He's from Alydar," Jude explained.

"And who's that?"

"Alydar finished second to Affirmed in all three Triple Crown races. He was probably the greatest horse in history *never* to win even a single Triple Crown race. He lost all three races to Affirmed by a total of less than two strides. The last race, the Belmont, was probably the greatest horse race of all time. Affirmed and Alydar battled neck and neck all the way down the stretch until Affirmed surged ahead right at the end to win the Belmont and go into the history books. No one knew, at the time, that decades would go by without another Triple Crown winner."

"And if Affirmed hadn't been racing that year …" I mused.

There was a sudden commotion on the grounds. Walkers for two of the horses had drifted too closely to each other on the grounds. Both horses had flared their nostrils, then one started to rear. The handlers struggled mightily to keep their two horses under control. Both horses were expending a great deal of energy in this prerace dance.

"So stupid." Jude shook his head. "Their handlers should know better, though it hardly matters with those two—they're both going off at forty or fifty to one." He glanced over at our horse, walking off by itself, away from the other horses. It looked regal.

"Ours looks different—calmer," I said.

"That's because I hired the best training staff in the racing world. I spared no expense. We have the best trainer in the business and the hottest jockey right now."

"I know." I laughed. "Not that it matters."

Jude smiled at me as we leaned casually on the railing that surrounded the parade grounds. "But to answer your question—yes, if Affirmed hadn't been racing that year, there's a good chance that Alydar would have won the Triple Crown. It was just his bad luck that he came to the track the same year as Affirmed."

Now my brother's actions were starting to make sense. I knew Jude and his knack for telling a great story that everyone understood at a gut level. "That's why you named him Alydar's Ghost," I said softly. "If he wins today ..."

"Then every sportswriter in America will bring back that historic duel between Affirmed and Alydar," Jude said, his voice rising with excitement. "It will be a huge story."

"Like Alydar riding again." I chuckled.

"And winning the Triple Crown, like he should have a generation ago."

"And you're sure he's going to win?" I pressed.

"We're making some necessary moves to make certain." Jude looked off to his left. "See that horse, the one with the white and blue colors? That's the favorite on the board right now. It's won three graded stakes in a row and is going off at six to five right now."

I started to raise my hand to point at the horse.

Jude grabbed my arm and held it in place. "Don't. That would call attention to what's about to happen."

We turned our attention back to the horse with blue and white. Most of the onlookers were still watching the two long shots prance and rear on the opposite side of the parade grounds. So we were among the few who saw a big, ugly, black vulture-like bird swoop down from the peak of one of the nearby barns. It almost collided with the horse in blue and white before veering off, heading away from the grounds, and disappearing behind another barn. The horse spooked terribly and then stumbled just as badly. The walker panicked, and the horse stumbled again before the walker was able to get him under control again. Even from here, I could see what had happened. The horse's right foreleg had hit the ground awkwardly. It was now favoring it slightly as it walked.

"Takes care of that," Jude said, nodding to no one in particular.

"Just like that?" I asked.

"Racehorses have delicate legs. It doesn't take much to cause trouble to them."

I already knew the answer, but I asked it anyway. "And I'm assuming that wasn't a bird? And that you have more of those things waiting in the wings to make certain events go your way?"

Jude didn't answer the question but pushed back from the railing. "Okay, ten minutes to post. Time to take our place in our celebrity owners' box and get ready to watch history being made."

Alydar's Ghost won the Kentucky Derby by three lengths, going away. The prerace favorite, the horse with the blue and white colors, pulled up a bit lame about three-quarters of the way through the race and finished well back in the pack. Two of the other favorites had what the handicappers called "rough trips"—one veered wide for some unexplained reason around the far turn and a second stumbled against the railing without provocation. There was no race inquiry afterward.

Just as Jude had predicted, every single sportswriter seized immediately on the storyline. *ALYDAR RIDES AGAIN!* screamed the headline on the top of the *Daily Racing Form*. There was massive speculation about whether Alydar's Ghost would right the wrong that so many racing fans still remembered from the Affirmed-Alydar duels.

And Jude was right there at every step, calmly telling the story about how he'd been enthralled with the hope—the mere possibility—that he'd once seen in the young yearling at the Keeneland sales.

"I fell in love with Alydar's Ghost the moment I saw him," Jude told the writer for *Sports Illustrated*. "And I just believed, in my heart, that Alydar's Ghost might bring back that long-lost glory from 1978."

"So you truly believed that Alydar's Ghost might be the first Triple Crown winner in a generation?" the sportswriter asked him.

"I thought Alydar's Ghost could right that wrong," Jude said confidently. "And it might just happen."

When Alydar's Ghost won the Preakness two weeks later, the story broke out of the sports world and on to the front pages of nearly every newspaper in the world. With Jude providing colorful quotes along the way, the story about how Alydar's Ghost just might "right the wrong" done by Affirmed way back in 1978 launched itself to the top of the public's mind.

By the time the Belmont Stakes arrived, Jude's winsome, smiling face had appeared in hundreds of publications alongside pictures of the now-famous descendant of Alydar. Tens of millions of people tuned in to the Belmont, nearly all hoping that Alydar's Ghost would win and "right the wrong."

There were so many photographers at the finish line of the Belmont on race day that they had to bring in rows of bleachers to accommodate them. Everyone wanted to be there when Alydar's Ghost crossed the finish line first.

When they announced the horses on the track, most of the photographers turned their cameras skyward toward the owners' boxes to capture Jude waving happily at the crowd below.

And when Alydar's Ghost won the Belmont Stakes to become the first Triple Crown winner in a generation, Jude immediately announced, live on the network covering the race, that he would donate both the race purse as well as the proceeds from the Triple Crown purse that hadn't been claimed since 1978 to the International Red Cross efforts in parts of the sub-Saharan that had been dealing with a three-year drought. The kid billionaire was now the quite-famous owner of a Triple Crown winner—the owner who'd found the horse to "right the wrong" as it rode to triumph and into the history books.

In one shining moment, Jude had inexplicably, seemingly against all odds, used a horse named after a famous, distant, losing legend to catapult himself into the public consciousness. It was, as Jude said, "One heckuva story."

# Chapter Nineteen

"It's called the American Redoubt," Frank Gore told me over the phone.

I was standing outside a coffee shop on the outskirts of Bozeman. Jagged mountain peaks framed the lower end of a sky that seemed bluer than I thought possible. The natural landscape literally made one stop and stare. "Redoubt?" I asked him. "Like doubting again?"

"No, nothing like that," Frank said, laughing. "It's a military term. It's like a fort or a defensive system that's actually outside a larger fort—an earth or stone barrier designed to slow down enemies as they approach the actual fort."

"A fort outside a bigger fort?" I was confused.

"You have to go back in time a bit," Frank explained. "Back to when forts were important, and you wanted to keep approaching armies from laying siege to it. They built additional barriers— redoubts—out of stone or brick that extended the outer perimeter of the fort itself. Redoubts could also serve as last resorts, a place of retreat in the event that the fort fell."

"Not much good today, considering that no one builds forts anymore ..."

"Hold that thought," Frank said enigmatically. "There's a place I want you to visit. It may surprise you a bit. But the concept of a redoubt has changed now that we're in a time of modern warfare, where sieges don't mean all that much in the military. Nowadays, the concept of a redoubt has more to do with a place where the remnant forces of a nation can withdraw and continue to defend themselves once the main battles have been lost. It can also be a place where these remnants pre-position themselves because they believe the main battle will be lost."

"Where would you find these … national redoubts?"

"They tend to spring up without any planning," Frank said. "When military forces realize that they've lost or that they're about to be overrun, they fall back to a mountainous region or a peninsula with fewer borders where they can more easily defend themselves and wait. That's the simplest way to think of it."

"I see," I said thoughtfully. "It's why al Qaeda hid in the mountains in and around Pakistan? That's the concept of a redoubt?"

"Yes and no. Al Qaeda wasn't a remnant force holding out to try to preserve their national independence—it's a loose confederation of jihadists and terrorist cells. But the redoubt concept is still roughly the same there—you fall back to a mountainous region where you're harder to find and where it's easier to defend yourself."

I looked out at the mountain peaks off in the distance. "So this … American Redoubt? That's the concept here? People moving out West to places like this because they believe it's a safe haven, a retreat, where they can survive the coming apocalypse?"

"Yes, in theory," Frank said. "It was a concept created some years ago, about a place where patriots could flee and establish a retreat— a redoubt—because they believed that America was so severely in decline that defeat and chaos were inevitable."

"Like a final holdout for families who believe that the dollar will crash, that financial chaos and martial law will descend in the United States, and that they will be ensconced in a place where they can withstand the societal upheavals?"

"Exactly." I could almost sense Frank smiling at the other end of the line. We'd had a number of these sorts of conversations since

I'd begun to explore the hidden parts of America that I'd never even known existed. I could never tell how much of what Frank was telling me he actually believed in.

"So where, exactly, is this American Redoubt?"

"It's mostly in just five states in the west—Montana, Wyoming, Idaho, and then just the eastern parts of Oregon and Washington, away from the big cities where the liberals have taken over."

"Yeah, right." I laughed. "There are Second Amendment patriots in Oregon and Washington?"

"You'd be surprised," Frank said. "But mostly the American Redoubt is largely confined to communities throughout just the first three states I mentioned—and especially in places like Idaho and Montana."

"So where do you live, Frank?" I asked him gently. "You've never said."

"And I won't—not to you and not to anyone else. The last thing I want is for hundreds of families to show up on my front lawn when your brother isn't around and the dollar finally collapses. They can find their own places."

"Yeah, they just need to read OTG?"

"Exactly. Has everything they'll need to get situated."

"But you're out here, somewhere in the American Redoubt?"

"That's a safe assumption," Frank replied. "And you could probably find me if you tried really hard. But I'd encourage you not to. I have somewhere else that I think you'll find a whole lot more interesting."

"Before we get there, though, I was curious," I said thoughtfully. "You've read Ayn Rand, right? Her book *Atlas Shrugged?*"

"Of course," Frank said. "We all have—those of us who value our freedom and don't trust the government to run the economy."

"So how does all of that square with the American Redoubt? The Second Amendment. Christian militias? Libertarians who want to abolish the Federal Reserve? They're all jumbled together, now that I've been around talking to folks. It's all built on a flimsy house of cards that fears a strong, centralized national government. I don't see any common ground between Christian patriots, as you call them, and libertarian worshippers at the altar of Ayn Rand. They have almost nothing in common other than a distrust of big government."

"That distrust is a pretty powerful bond, wouldn't you say?"

"Yeah, I guess," I admitted. "It's a powerful thing, bordering on raw hate, racism just beneath the surface, and extreme paranoia in plenty of the places I've visited in the last few weeks. But I still don't see how they coexist. I don't see any realistic way in which Galt's Gulch could exist out here in what you call the American Redoubt."

"Which is precisely why I want you to visit a place," Frank said. "I'll let them know you're headed their way. They'll let you in—based on my recommendation to the director—and show you the ropes. They'll give you a tour others wouldn't ordinarily see or even realize is there. And we'll talk afterward. I think things will become a bit clearer after you've been there."

"Will I find the Christian Brigades there?"

"Patience." Frank laughed. "First things first."

I took a deep breath, taking in big gulps of the cool, crisp air in what was arguably one of the most breathtaking places on the planet. "Okay, fine," I said a bit testily. "I'll wait. So where am I going?"

"It's called the Fortress. You can drive there from Bozeman, up toward Kalispell and the northwest part of Montana."

"And it's called that—the Fortress?"

"It is, though it isn't a city or an official name," Frank said. "It's just their name for the community of idealists and believers who've settled there."

"Christian believers?"

"You'll see soon enough. It's a self-selected group of believers. They don't exclude by race or religion. Anyone is welcome—if they are interested in what the community stands for."

"But they're all white, conservative Christians?" I pressed.

"Ask them yourself when you get there," Frank said. "There were two such places in the news a few years ago when the concept was first proposed at the heart of the American Redoubt. There's a place to the west, in the mountains at the edge of Oregon, called the Citadel. It was proposed as a gated community for Christians who wanted the ability to trust their neighbors when lawlessness and chaos descended. Guns were not only allowed—they were welcomed. In fact, the Citadel built a munitions and ammo factory inside the walls to make certain they wouldn't run out."

"Inside the walls of the place? They make their own guns and ammo? And DHS allows it?"

"Sure, why not?" Frank said. "Guns have to be manufactured somewhere, and that's as good a place as any."

"I'll bet they feel safe at the Citadel," I joked.

"They do. Everyone knows their neighbors at the Citadel. It costs a pretty penny to buy a lot there and build your own place on the grounds. It's a real gated community with hefty dues. They run a tight ship."

"You've been there?"

"Many times," Frank said. "They invite me in to speak there quite often, in fact."

"So the Fortress is like that—like the Citadel?"

Frank paused briefly. "They were lumped together in the press for a bit. The media has an awfully bad habit of that—not discerning, I mean. They sound the same, they're both in the American Redoubt, and they're both a bit secluded and walled off from society. So they must be similar. But people forgot about it eventually. Now that the Fortress is largely built out and thriving, they don't go out of their way to advertise themselves. But people who need to know about it find the place, visit, and even settle there."

"They sure sound similar," I offered.

"They aren't. But I'll leave it at that. Go see for yourself. They're expecting you."

"Are you there, Frank? At the Fortress?" I asked.

"You are relentless, aren't you?"

I chuckled. "So I've been told."

"Go see the Fortress for yourself. I'll try to answer your questions after you've been there. But I think the place will make sense to you all on its own."

# Chapter Twenty

I was twenty-seven when I first met Singen Prithar. I knew immediately that he was different than the other regents who had grown to play such prominent roles in my brother's life. Singen had a way about him that set him apart. He seemed more certain of himself, less afraid of upstaging Jude while he was in his presence.

Singen did have the same cold, forbidding austereness as the other regents, as if he were incapable of smiling. But I could sense a higher level of intelligence or willfulness in Singen than I'd detected in the other regents.

We met first at the opulent office Jude had taken for himself at the southern end of Central Park after his bet against the yen. I'd never asked him, but I believe Jude had invited me to his office just so he could show off Singen to me, like he was a prized acquisition.

After Jude's bet against the yen, it had become apparent that it was rather silly of me to keep working at *The Herald-Sun* in Durham covering local politics in North Carolina.

We were now worth billions and had crept our way onto various lists of America's wealthiest individuals. It was becoming progressively harder for me to maintain my anonymity, and I finally gave up on it altogether and moved to New York.

But I didn't take my brother's advice. I didn't just use our vast wealth to buy my way into a prominent position as the publisher of a media outlet in the city. Instead, I simply took a job as a reporter for a national New York-based magazine that was rapidly resigning itself to obsolescence and began to write about the environment.

"Get over here," Jude texted me one afternoon shortly after I'd moved to New York and begun my new job.

"Why?" I'd texted back.

"I have news," he'd written.

"What?" I texted back.

"You'll see," he wrote. "Plus, I have a new office I want you to see. It can be yours, too."

"No, thanks. Have one already," I'd texted back.

I was curious, though, and took the subway over to the office. I got off at the 59th Street stop and walked two blocks east to his office. The desk guard gave me a curious look when I signed my last name in the visitor's log—likely because I looked like my brother—but didn't say anything. When I got off the elevator on the forty-third floor—the top floor of the building—I understood why.

An enormous sign—Asher Enterprises—was posted over the top of the glass double doors to the entrance to Jude's new office. The face-recognition camera set casually over the top of the sign must have picked me up instantly, since the doors swung open before I'd reached them. I kept walking and entered the offices.

A stunningly attractive brunette receptionist left the black marble desk near the center of the foyer and walked toward me. "Welcome, sir," she said with a brilliant smile. "We've been expecting you, Mr. Asher."

"Please, just call me Thomas," I said quickly. As I always did with attractive women, I did my best to just look her directly in the eyes and not let my own wander.

"As you wish, sir," she said demurely. "But Mr. Asher—your brother—wanted me to let you know that you are welcome here whenever you'd like." She looked over one shoulder, down a hallway. "In fact, you have your own office, which you may use as you see fit."

"No need," I said with a smile. "I'm fine."

"Very well. Your brother informed me that you would decline the offer. But he also wanted me to emphasize that you are welcome to consider this your office as well, whenever you'd like."

"Duly noted." I had to give it to Jude. He was persistent, if nothing else.

She turned and beckoned. "If you will follow me?"

As we walked down the hallway, I glanced at the carefully placed artwork on the walls. They appeared to be originals, not copies.

Despite myself, I almost gasped when we entered Jude's new conference room. A boardroom table that could easily accommodate dozens of people dominated the center of the room. But what took my breath away was the view—an enormous plate-glass window that looked over Central Park.

I walked to the window and stood there, admiring the view. The park below was a vast green ocean in the middle of the city's concrete jungle. From up here, with a view like this, looking out over some of the most expensive real estate in the world at the center of one of the most iconic cities in history, it was easy to imagine what it might be like to be a lord of the earth—sitting atop a very high mountain, gazing down at the kingdom below.

"Spectacular, isn't it?"

I turned, expecting to see my brother. Instead, I found myself looking across the huge conference room at someone I'd never seen before. Dark-haired and olive-skinned, he leaned casually against the side of the doorway.

"It is," I said. "I can't even imagine what it costs Jude for this view."

"Oh, I'm sure you can imagine it—even if you choose not to think about it all that much," he answered evenly. He pushed off the door frame and made his way across the cavernous room. His well-tailored suit swished faintly as he walked, the hard leather soles of his Italian shoes making a slight tapping as he crossed the wooden floor. His eyes flashed with a dark intensity as he extended a hand. "Singen Prithar. I am your brother's new counsel here at Asher Enterprises."

The question formed in my mind, unasked. "Counsel?" I asked instead. "Which means what exactly?"

"Whatever your brother wishes, to be candid," Singen said. "I am here to serve."

"I see." I nodded. "Speaking of Jude, is he here?"

"He is," Singen said. "But he wanted us to speak first, privately. I, especially, felt that it was long past time for us to get acquainted properly. Jude agreed. And to answer the question you have not asked—yes, I am one of *those things*, as you occasionally refer to us."

I tried my best to keep my emotions in check. It wasn't easy. I'd never been comfortable around any of the regents. Jude had always respected that and had never really asked me to interact with them. I wondered why this particular regent had emerged from my brother's shadow. And yet, even as this question formed, I already knew the answer.

Singen was clearly different. He was no mere servant. He was a leader. Of what, exactly, I couldn't say. But whoever, or whatever, he was, Singen was long accustomed to commanding respect and getting what he wanted in the world. Every aspect of his being clearly said so. No words were required.

"Singen Prithar. That's a fairly unusual name."

"I borrowed some German and some Indian," he replied. "So, yes, it is a bit unusual. But it has a nice ring, doesn't it?"

I wasn't entirely sure how to answer a question like that. Perhaps it was rhetorical. I moved away from the window and took a seat at the conference table. Singen sat as well, his back to the window and, thus, the spectacular view of Central Park. He focused his gaze on me—studiously avoiding the view behind him—as we took our seats.

"What was the news that Jude had for me?" I asked when we were seated.

Singen leaned forward slightly. His eyes never left mine. "It is time for his childhood—for *your* childhood—to pass. There is a time for childish things. That time has ended. Jude now realizes this, and he wanted to convey that to you."

"I'm not sure what that means, exactly."

"It means that Jude has put the childish things he's been preoccupied with for the past few years behind him," Singen said earnestly. "He's had his fill. He's seen and done more than enough to satisfy his curiosity about such things. Winning the Triple Crown—and all the attendant fame that came with it—clearly slaked whatever thirst he had for that sort of exposure to the public."

"So no more celebrities? No more lavish parties? He isn't planning on buying an NFL franchise to go after the Super Bowl, or perhaps a NASCAR team? No more late-night jet-setting to remote corners of the globe on a whim?"

"Not unless it is *necessary*. Not unless there is a reason to be seen or heard in some part of society. He learned some valuable lessons during the Triple Crown incident—some that he'd anticipated, and some that he had not."

I nodded. I'd wondered when Jude would grow tired of such ventures, though I'd expected it at some point. "So was this *his* idea—or yours?"

"You know," Singen answered slowly, "I've always told Jude that there was much more to you just beneath the surface than he knew. We've had many conversations to that effect. I've often said he was underestimating you—and what you're capable of at the right moment."

I chose to ignore the faint praise. Instead, I pointed out, "You didn't answer the question."

"Your brother has come to realize that it is time to put childish things away. That is how I would answer that question."

"I see." I nodded. "So it *was* your idea."

"It is Jude's wish. And, as always, I will honor that wish and do my best to help him progress along the path that he's chosen."

I'd often wondered how I would react in a conversation like this. I'd avoided it, even dreaded it at times. Yet, strangely, it was nothing like I'd expected—at all. I wasn't afraid of Singen or intimidated by him and what he represented. Mostly, I was just curious. So I decided to clear up a few things.

"So when we were kids at the farm in Waterford?" I asked. "And something that looked awfully similar at Churchill Downs?"

Singen almost smiled. "Very elemental creatures, actually. They cater to basic needs and wants. They are able to take very direct orders, on singular missions."

"So they're like, what … starter kits?"

"Something like that."

"But Jude graduated from those?"

"Quite rapidly," Singen explained. "He had no real interest in them and wanted much more than they had to offer. In fact, once he grasped what they were all about, he nearly stopped calling on them."

"And the regents, the ones I've seen hanging around managing his affairs and keeping track of him when he's out in public?"

"Much greater awareness," Singen said. "Capable of controlling a variety of factors and complexity. Your brother saw that almost immediately. It was much more to his liking, intellectually. He was always innately curious about how much control he could exert over the natural environment around him—and just how far that control could extend beyond his reach."

"And you?"

"Not a regent—at least, not in the sense that you know."

Something had nagged me for years, so I asked the question. "I've wondered for a while now—can you see my thoughts? Do you know what I'm thinking?"

Singen smiled. "It isn't all that difficult to know what anyone is thinking, really, at any given time. Words convey your thoughts, for instance. So do your body movements and, of course, your actions. But, no, I cannot see your thoughts—unless you wish me to?"

"No, that's fine," I said, satisfied. "It's generally what I'd always assumed. But I was still curious. So. What are you good at then? What is your … area of expertise?"

Singen gave me a curious look. "Is that really what you're interested in? My area of expertise? My domain? You don't wish to know more than that? You don't wish to come to terms with principalities and powers, understand the nature of the human species and civilization?"

"I'll leave aside the meaning of life, for now, I think," I said calmly. "I prefer to figure those sorts of things on my own time, in my own way. So will you tell me your area of expertise?"

"Very well," Singen said with an easy, practiced shrug. "I have been—I should say, I am—an expert in the nature of the wealth of nations. It is what Jude absolutely requires now at this moment, and I am delighted to help him with that."

"That's next for my brother? He wants to learn how to direct the wealth of nations—as opposed to just trying his hand at side bets that grow our bank accounts at Asher Enterprises?"

"Among other things," Singen said in a controlled manner. "From great wealth, great power is derived, after all—both for individuals as well as nations. I daresay that very few quite understand that. They don't truly understand monetary systems, yet they know how to spend money. They hear about the Federal Reserve and somehow believe it is a part of their national government."

I scanned the lavish boardroom again. "So this is Jude's new playground. And what will he learn here?"

"How wealth can, in fact, serve as an instrument of influence, not simply as a means to buy or consume what one desires," Singen said. "The wealth of nations is, truly, a mysterious thing that can be manipulated and controlled if you know the right levers and authorities. It is, dare I say, much like the mysterious hand of God."

"An interesting concept," I mused. "And it is Jude who wishes to come to terms with this art—this wealth of nations?"

"It is a lesson that he does, indeed, wish to learn."

"Yet it almost certainly serves your ends, whatever those might happen to be?" I asked carefully. "I hope you don't take offense at that question."

"I take no offense whatsoever. I serve Jude," he answered calmly. "It is a high, time-honored calling."

"I see. So you receive nothing in return?"

"I receive the satisfaction of a lesson well taught and an apt student who learns quickly."

"There is nothing else you ask of him in return? Truly nothing at all?" I studied Singen's reaction as I asked the question. He paused for a long time, clearly weighing his words and his response quite carefully.

*Presumably he can't lie,* I thought. *But he can use words as weapons and twist them to suit some aim or another. But, in the end, he has to tell some version of the truth. Interesting.*

"Jude wishes to learn these lessons, and I am willing to serve as his mentor in this endeavor," Singen responded. "That certainly seems sufficient motivation on both ends." He quickly changed direction then, without really answering my question. "These are lessons you can learn as well," he offered. "There is no reason you shouldn't profit from this knowledge, if you seek it."

"But I don't seek it," I said. "I never have. It's what Jude wants. It's not what I'm interested in, at any price."

"Are you so certain of that?" Singen asked intently.

"Only fools are certain," I replied. "However, I *do* know that this particular path may be Jude's—but it is not mine."

# Chapter Twenty-One

Just for fun, I checked the classified ads in the daily newspaper in Bozeman before setting off in my rental car for Kalispell. I had clear directions to the Fortress from Frank, and it would be a scenic drive up into the mountains. But I was also curious, and the classified section of the paper satisfied that curiosity.

It was littered with multiple ads for self-sufficient homes that ran on energy sources not connected to the power grid and estate companies that seemed to specialize in selling precisely these sorts of properties to white, Christian families looking to get away, no questions asked.

The properties were spread throughout the entire region, within a relatively easy drive from the city. Bozeman was, in a sense, like Grand Central station for those wishing to move out to the American West and then literally take themselves and their families off the grid.

Bozeman was quite possibly one of the most interesting cities I'd ever come across. I could easily see myself living here. The land was welcoming and gorgeous. Yet, just beneath the surface was a rather secretive subculture of families who genuinely believed that American society was on the edge of collapse and who wanted to be as far away from that imminent collapse as they could be.

I could also hear it in casual conversation in coffee shops, gas stations, and fast-food restaurants. People said they felt safe in Bozeman and the surrounding areas. They didn't worry about crime or getting mugged or robbed. They could safely carry their guns with them in public and didn't worry about second glances. It was all very curious to me.

Before setting off for Kalispell and the Fortress, though, I called Sandy. I was curious what she thought of Jude's Senate campaign. But, mostly, I wanted to hear her voice. It was a strange sensation for me—this desire to hear the voice of someone I'd come to rely on and even trust a little. I wasn't entirely sure I knew what that meant.

"I miss you," I said without announcing myself as soon as she picked up.

I thought I could hear a catch in her breath. "Where *are* you, exactly, Thomas?" she asked a moment later. "And how long will you be gone?"

"I'm in Bozeman, Montana. God's country. Come join me. I'll send a jet for you."

"No, you will most emphatically *not* send a jet for me," she said firmly. "I'm busy right now with two new clients. I like them, and I'm having fun. So you keep your jet and get yourself back here to the city. I miss you, too."

It was something I'd discovered about her, somewhat by accident, once I'd allowed the relationship to grow beyond the embryonic stage. She didn't really have much use for my wealth. She didn't mind it, of course. She didn't decline a nice date on the town. But she had no lust for it. That had surprised me.

I'd thought, at first, that Sandy skated on the surface and didn't pay all that much attention to the deeper aspects of life. I'd assumed she was interested in the nicer things in life and was therefore interested in the material things that wealth could buy. I was wrong on both counts.

Sandy had made it herself, on her own. She'd paid her way through college when her parents told her they couldn't help. Her first few jobs were secured on sheer guts and tenacity, and she'd worked like a dog to pay off her student loans on time. She'd even managed to become an executive vice president at a good Madison Avenue ad agency at an early age. Sandy was an independent, professional woman who had succeeded in one of the toughest cities in the world—and she was quietly proud of that accomplishment. I'd discounted it at first, mostly because I didn't really know her or what that meant. But I knew it now. I respected it. And I missed her.

"You sure?" I asked. "It's breathtaking out here. The mountains just seem to claw their way toward the sky. You can see in all directions for miles and miles."

"I'm sure," she answered. "So what are you doing in Bozeman?"

"I'm about to find out." I told her a bit of my conversation with Frank and that I was heading to someplace called the Fortress. I asked her about Jude's Senate race, which was only a few weeks away now.

"He's going to win easily," she reasoned. "The *Times* just ran a story on some of the latest polls. It doesn't look like it'll even be close."

"I guess his luck keeps holding."

"Doesn't look like luck to me," Sandy replied. "The ads he's been running are brilliant. Absolutely brilliant. Every ad agency in the city is wondering where the concepts came from."

"What are they?" I asked. For reasons I obviously couldn't explain to Sandy, I'd never asked Jude what he would tell the public about his reasons for running for the Senate. I knew why he was running, just as I'd known why he'd taken every other path in his life.

"It's a story," she explained. "He's been telling the story of his life, in chapters, for the last four weeks. No ad is the same. Every spot tells a completely new and different part of his life. People are going online to find the ads that they missed, like they're episodes of a television series.

He uses celebrities and famous events and icons in each of them. But not in a pretentious or obnoxious way. They're simply part of the fabric of who he is. They relate to what he says is the best of America, what he wants Americans to celebrate about their way of life. Thomas, I have to say—honestly—they're inspiring. I'm inspired by them—by him. They make you want to go out and knock on doors for him, propel him into office. I don't know any other way to say it. He just looks like a leader—one whom we always seemed to be waiting for but who never actually showed up on the scene."

"You do know that this is my twin brother you're talking about here, right?" I chided her. "So I guess you're going to vote for him?"

She laughed. I liked the sound of it and wished I were there beside her to hear it. "Yeah, I guess I'll vote for him—even if he is ugly."

"Hey! Be nice."

"You know," she said, lowering her voice, "you've always been so circumspect about your brother. I know that something happened between you two years ago and that you don't really talk much anymore. I guess that's why I've been so interested in these ads that sort of tell the story of Jude. It's been fun to follow along. And I think other people feel that way too. It's like he's giving people a chance to peek inside his life a bit."

"Well, good for him," I said, trying to keep the edge out of my voice. "I'm glad Jude has found a way to tell his life story. But I can assure you—it's the story he wants you to hear, the way he wants you to hear it." I stopped. I really didn't want Sandy to hear the bitterness I harbored.

"What is it?" she asked. "What is it about your brother that troubles you so much that you can't even speak about it to me or anyone else?"

I almost told her, right then. But I knew how silly it would sound, how thoroughly and utterly insane it would seem to her. People do things for all kinds of personal, self-centered reasons. Everyone is the center of their own universe, the star of their own, personal drama. My brother had just taken that up a few levels—quite a few levels.

"Oh, it's nothing, Sandy. Really. I just know Jude well, better than anyone. And he's not perfect, no matter how it comes off to other people. That's all."

"None of us are perfect," she said quietly. "We all make mistakes. I'm sure your brother is no different."

"Oh, he's different," I replied. "And he knows what he's doing. But maybe we can just leave it at that. Is that all right, for now?"

"For now. But someday you'll tell me, right? You'll tell me what happened and why you and your brother don't talk anymore?"

I paused. "Yeah, someday. But not now, not over the phone."

"I mean it," she said, her tone softer. "I want to know a lot more about you, in all ways. I like where we're going. And part of that is knowing the hard parts of your life—not just the easy ones. I want you to feel safe with me."

I closed my eyes, imagining what Sandy looked like at that moment at the other end of the line. "I will," I vowed. "I promise. But, first, I need to get to the bottom of this journey I find myself on."

"Come home soon, okay?"

"I will. Soon."

As I drove toward Kalispell, I found myself wondering why, exactly, Frank Gore had decided to trust me with this journey into the heart of his own carefully managed world. Frank was no intellectual slouch. I'd grown to admire his dry wit during some of our late-night conversations as I recovered from the day's troubles in a motel room.

Frank seemed to genuinely enjoy my questions. He never took offense to anything I asked, no matter how abrupt it might have seemed. People told reporters all types of things that they shouldn't tell a soul. But it wasn't that way with Frank. He knew precisely what he was doing by opening up to me.

I concluded, on my drive to the Fortress, that Frank probably wanted to see if someone who was not from his conspiracy-minded world could take a hard, objective look at his life's mission and not reject it out of hand. I was that witness, and Frank wanted to see if he could convince me, both through words and a peek inside the machinery.

I spied the Fortress from miles off. It wasn't hidden—not by any means. In fact, anyone driving north and west toward the mountains could clearly see it halfway up the gently rising eastern slope of what ultimately becomes one of the tallest mountains in this part of the country. The turrets and towers atop a very large retaining wall had seemingly been carved right out of the side of the mountain. They were impossible to miss as a car approached the foothills leading upward.

There was no way at all to take the Fortress by surprise—not unless you planned on storming the place with a series of military-style helicopters capable of literally dropping out of the sky from the west and over the top of the mountain ridge that towered over the top.

No, to get to the Fortress, you had to drive along a road that wound back and forth for nearly an hour. Anyone watching from the highest points along the wall around the Fortress could see approaching cars the entire time. It was literally impossible to sneak up on the Fortress.

As I made my way back and forth along the switchbacks, I wondered how many eyes were watching my progress at that moment, weapons at their sides. I assumed there were at least a few watching me make my way to this place, given that Frank had told them that I was on my way. No matter. I'd deal with whatever I found when I arrived. I wasn't worried.

When I made the final turn on the last switchback, road signs told me to slow to fifteen miles an hour. I slowed the car and came to a halt several minutes later in front of one of the more elaborate gates I'd seen.

The architects had taken the notion of a gated community and pumped it full of steroids. The gate had triple hinges on both sides and large metal poles that slid up and down at the center of the gate into drilled holes in the cement beneath the gate. There was a call box off to the driver's side of what had become a narrow, one-way street entering the compound.

I laughed out loud when I read the words etched into the plate at the top of the gate: *Lord Acton Gate*. That was clearly someone's idea of an inside joke. Lord Acton, a Christian and libertarian in some ways, was most famous for defining the power of the state. "Power tends to corrupt, and absolute power tends to corrupt absolutely," Acton had written.

I punched the button on the call box and waited. "Welcome, Mr. Asher," said a calm, soothing voice from a speaker on the side of the box. "We've been expecting you. The gate will open in just a moment, and you'll be able to drive inside. Someone will be there to greet you."

I didn't wonder how they'd known it was me. But I did wonder what might be waiting for me on the other side. So I decided to ask. "If I might, could you tell me who exactly will be there to greet me when I arrive?"

"Why, the director, of course," said the voice. "We've been expecting you for some time—for days, in fact, as word traveled about your inquiries and questions. All roads like the one you are traveling tend to arrive here eventually."

The gate swung open then. I drove in.

# Chapter Twenty-Two

Jude made his big move shortly before our thirtieth birthdays. It had always been a running joke between the two of us. "No one takes you seriously before you turn thirty, so you might as well try everything you can until then."

That wasn't true, of course. But it made for a good story at dinner parties and afforded Jude some public leeway to experiment a bit in the marketplace and financial world.

By our thirtieth birthdays, Asher Enterprises had become one of the five wealthiest private companies in America. Every so often, I asked Jude whether there was ever any need to take the company public, especially as we grew more successful.

"Why?" he'd answer. "So that we have to file quarterly reports with the SEC, hold inane quarterly earnings reports for the financial media who ask stupid questions, take a short-term view of how to grow wealth, and generally make ourselves insane each quarter to show consistent growth?"

With Singen's steady hand at the wheel, Jude and Asher Enterprises became quite adept at buying entire companies and turning them into industry leaders in a very short period of time. Because it was a private company that owned other big companies, Asher Enterprises was free to maneuver easily between widely different industries with seemingly different markets and objectives. There were no shareholders looking over our shoulders, second-guessing our intentions, motives, or strategies.

Yet in those acquisitions, Jude somehow managed to find the most unusual joint ventures that benefitted the different companies in Asher Enterprises' portfolio of companies. It was almost as if he had inside knowledge about where to look for value, how to buy a potential industry leader right before that industry exploded, or how to reach across industries to create wealth through nothing more than synergy.

For instance, Asher Enterprises once bought a railroad line teetering on the edge of bankruptcy because it was easier and cheaper to ship goods by truck or barge. Railroads seemed an archaic thing of the past. This particular rail line ran from Canada, through the Dakotas and the American West, and then down to a dilapidated waterfront in Houston, Texas. There seemed no good reason to buy the railroad line, because there was no compelling need to ship on the rail lines.

At the same time, Asher Enterprises purchased nearly three million separate leases on big parcels of land all throughout the Dakotas and much of Canada. Because we were private, we didn't have to announce it publicly. We just bought the leases and held them.

Jude then met with the economic minister of Israel and created a joint venture to bring a newly developed technology to commercial scale—a technology that allowed a drilling development company to bring oil trapped in shale rock to the surface without using water and fracturing technology.

And when the State Department in the United States denied a controversial pipeline that was supposed to carry oil from parts of Canada to American ports, Asher Enterprises stepped in and offered cheap rail service. It also immediately turned the dilapidated Houston waterfront property into a line of refineries almost overnight.

In one fell swoop, Jude had created a new cradle-to-grave industry that used leading-edge technology to bring what was called "tight oil" economically and efficiently from both the Dakotas and Canada, ship it directly by a rail line that Asher Enterprises owned and had seemingly built to directly serve this new venture, refine the oil in new plants at the port in Houston, and then sell it directly to China to fuel their energy-hungry economy in a deal that Jude and Singen negotiated directly with the Chinese president.

Because Asher Enterprises wasn't required to report any of this activity to the SEC, shareholders, or the financial press, much of it had gone unnoticed. But the financial press was clearly starting to take notice and had begun to write stories about how and why Asher Enterprises always seemed to guess correctly at critical moments. Jude's ability to know things seemed prescient to them. If they only knew.

The financial press also tried to guess at our net worth. They always got it completely wrong, underestimating our true net worth by a considerable margin. What none of the reporters could possibly see were all of the other activities where Singen was mentoring Jude. There were the infrequent, big bets against various currencies that always seemed timed just right. But there were other things that seemingly made no sense to anyone, yet they created vast wealth because they were so thoroughly tied to the underlying economy of an individual country. Jude was, in fact, learning how to control the wealth of nations.

"Did you know that you can actually sell water?" Jude told me once. "It's more valuable than oil in some countries."

"How is that possible?" I'd asked him. The notion seemed a bit crazy. Water was free and abundant—or so I thought.

"A billion people in Southeast Asia depend on the monsoon season for their fresh water. When something happens to it, then things get disrupted. There are parts of China that struggle for water when the glaciers in the Himalayas change. Parts of Africa are in their fourth year of sustained droughts, so water has to be provided from other parts of the world to sustain their domestic agriculture. Water can be a commodity just like anything else."

Jude also explained how China had cornered the market on the ability to refine rare metals that were critical for everything from cell phones to advanced weapons systems. So Jude cut a deal with the Chinese president—his new best friend—and broke that monopoly. The White House and Pentagon, and every technology company in the world, were now in his debt.

"But the thing that really astounds me—and which I wouldn't even have guessed if Singen had not shown me how it was possible— is that we are literally able to pick up the debt of an entire country," Jude told me one evening as we stood admiring the view of Central Park from his office.

"An entire country? Like assuming the mortgage debt on a house?" I'd asked.

"Not a large country, mind you," Jude had said. "But, yes, it's not unlike taking over the mortgage payments on a house. The country starts writing checks to Asher Enterprises, with most of it being interest payments."

"So it really is a bit like a mortgage payment?"

"Yes, a bit like that, only at a *slightly* bigger level." He'd laughed.

"And if the country decides it doesn't want to pay the interest on that debt any longer?"

"Doesn't happen. We can always renegotiate or restructure. The payments keep coming at some level. No country wants to default on its debt. It prints money before coming to that. Either way, we're fine."

"And you always have Singen and the regents at your side," I'd said calmly.

"Yes," he'd said, smiling. "There is that as well. But, honestly, it amazes me that a private company, even one with the capital resources we now command, can actually cover the debt of an entire country. It's quite extraordinary."

Every so often, a reporter would ask me why I wasn't just running companies like my much more famous twin brother. I always replied with the same answer. "Not my thing. I like reporting and writing. It's what I want to do." Every reporter who ever asked me this question believed I was stark-raving mad. Who worked for a living as a scribe when they could own the barrels of ink? It made no sense to them.

In my heart, I knew that I'd have to give up the charade at some point and quit writing about things from the sidelines. But I wanted to hold on to my own world for as long as humanly possible. It wasn't something I could explain to anyone. I didn't want my brother's world. I wanted my own life. And, for now, that meant observing and writing about the natural world that my brother had no part in. I couldn't see an alternate path.

But all of this paled in comparison when Jude made his big bet right before our thirtieth birthday. I guess I should have seen it coming, if I'd thought about it at all. Whatever slim hope I'd harbored about maintaining a low profile in the world vanished in the face of the scrutiny that followed in the wake of Jude's bet.

Just as Asher Enterprises had taken over debt payments in several small countries, China had assumed a significant portion of the debt for the United States. I had no earthly idea how this was possible, but Singen clearly understood it. So, by extension, Jude did as well.

China had been trying for years to establish its own currency, the yuan, on world markets. That was one of the reasons China's leaders were more than happy to buy up so much of America's debt—it lent enormous credibility to the yuan. China even managed to pull a handful of countries away from the US financial orbit. But the dollar was still, in effect, the world's currency. Nothing China's leadership did seemed to change the equation between the yuan and the dollar.

Until Jude's bet. What I knew—because I'd sat in the boardroom with Jude and Singen for the pivotal meeting during which they made their decision—was that it was a willful, deliberate effort on Jude's part to push things to the point where such a bet was even possible. And I knew the effort Jude had gone through to make $2 billion by shorting Japan's currency had been only a trial run for this much larger bet.

It began with a series of joint deals with the Chinese president that linked the yuan to a series of debt instruments that Asher Enterprises now essentially controlled in countries on four continents. China then began to exert its influence in those areas, triggering further actions.

With Jude and Singen directing traffic and pulling levers, each of those countries then made their own seemingly independent decisions at the national level—all at the same time. The net effect was to cause a severe credit crunch on a global scale at a time when no one was willing to lend at that sort of scale. China sat on the sidelines for its own reasons—hoping the dollar would be crippled.

Which is precisely what began to happen. The result seemed to come out of nowhere, but I knew better. The world's financial press panicked all at once, reporting stories predicting hyperinflation in the United States if it was forced to print money to deal with the pressure on its own currency and manage the debt that China suddenly seemed unwilling or incapable of helping with.

But at the scariest possible moment in the looming, impending crash of the dollar, Jude entered the fray. In a series of daring, other-worldly bets that the global financial press covered as if it were a Hail Mary at the end of the Super Bowl with hundreds of millions watching, Jude took short positions directly against the Chinese yuan—and directly in support of the American dollar.

Jude, in effect, bet against the Chinese and in support of the Americans. While the press could only speculate on the consequences, their assumptions were essentially correct.

Just as he had when he'd shorted the Japanese yen, Jude essentially put nearly all of his many connections and joint ventures, as well as the now-considerable private holdings of Asher Enterprises, at risk in this one very large, very public bet that pitted the American dollar against the Chinese yuan.

It worked, as if by magic. The yuan slipped, and the dollar pulled out of its rapid, seemingly unstoppable descent. Jude had saved the American dollar from collapse.

All of the attendant catastrophes that may have occurred in the wake of such a collapse of the dollar were averted. The US housing market stabilized. Gold prices declined again. The Federal Reserve's board breathed a big sigh of relief. The secretary of treasury now had Jude on speed dial. All talk of the potential for rampant hyperinflation in the US market melted away.

If Alydar's Ghost's winning the Triple Crown had made Jude Asher a bit more known to the public, his dramatic bet to save the American dollar had established him as a global megastar. The question that a magazine headline had once asked as the dollar was crashing—"Can He Save Us?"—had been answered.

Jude had, quite literally, saved America from financial ruin with his one big bet. I wondered whether anyone, other than me, thought about how it might truly have all come to pass. And I wondered, too, what it meant.

# Chapter Twenty-Three

There was no military guard waiting for me once the gate opened and I was allowed to drive my rental car inside the Fortress. There were no storm troopers with blue helmets and AK-47s at their side; no cluster of police watching my movements; no snipers positioned atop the walls overlooking the public square just inside the one and only gate that allowed entrance to the city.

There was only an elderly, bespectacled man with white hair, a gray cardigan, faded blue chinos, and casual slip-on loafers sitting on a simple, wooden bench off to one side of the gate. I parked my rental car in one of the three outdoor parking slots clearly marked for visitors, locked the car, and walked across the open space to greet him.

It wasn't at all what I'd expected. But, honestly, I hadn't really known *what* to expect in the first place, so this was a perfectly fine greeting party. I decided not to wait around for niceties and dove right in.

"Lord Acton? Really? How many people here would understand that inside joke?"

"Not many would," the director said. He rose from the bench and took a small step toward me to greet me as I approached the bench. He held out his hand. "But those who *do* appreciate it are the ones I care about."

"So what will I find next as I walk in the town that only the literary and political intelligentsia might appreciate?"

The director smiled. "Well, we have a pub that the owner affectionately named Galt's Gulch. There's a Rearden's Restaurant. And, of course, we have Dagny's Dry Cleaners …"

"But I thought she left Galt's Gulch for New York City? John Galt went to find her and ended up boring everyone with a speech of some sort that went on for seventy pages, if I recall."

"She did. But that was a work of fiction—and we still need a dry cleaners here."

I'd done my homework on the director of the Fortress before arriving and found myself charmed by him almost instantly. Like the entranceway to the Fortress, he was nothing like I'd anticipated from his writings and the biographies that were littered across various websites. He wasn't nearly the monster some made him out to be.

Dr. Jeremy Simons had gotten his PhD in biochemistry from Harvard and had later developed the world's first commercially viable lab to grow human organs in animals. He'd then subsequently formed a hugely successful multinational corporation around the research. He'd been a pioneer in genetic engineering. His work on transgenic technology was truly revolutionary. Some speculated that if he'd had no constraints placed on him by national governments, he'd have easily been the first person to successfully clone a human being. He was that gifted.

But his work had also raised any number of ethical issues for nearly two decades. Were he and his lab creating new life forms and crossing species boundaries? Were there unintended consequences to human health by introducing transgenic organs into the world? Was it even ethical to mix and match human and animal DNA, no matter if the resulting organ saved a human life?

Depending on the commentator, Simons was either a medical savior who'd developed technology that extended thousands of lives—or an evil genius bent on corrupting the human species.

Early in his career, Dr. Simons had publicly and defiantly taken on his critics. He was adamant that medical science knew no limits or boundaries and that he had every right to experiment with transgenic genes and new species. "A chimera is a mythical creature. I'm not creating mythical creatures. I'm saving lives," he'd once said.

But the quote that had caused him immense pain—in response to a question about whether it was right to play God by creating new, transgenic species for commercial and medical purposes—was one I hoped to ask him about: "I'm not playing God, but I'm as close to that on earth as you're likely to find. And if I want to create a better species, beyond the human one, then so be it," he'd told a reporter from the *Financial Times* at a medical conference in London.

The reaction in certain circles was swift, and almost all of it universally negative. Christian pastors worldwide condemned him from the pulpit almost immediately. The backlash nearly ruined his company, and many of its most prominent backers walked away over the controversy.

He'd tried to repair the damage, but it had been nearly impossible to put the genie back in the bottle. Dr. Simons had, overnight, become known worldwide as the mad scientist playing God with no ethical boundaries. He was the "next Josef Mengele" as more than one columnist wrote. Dr. Simons had largely stopped talking to the media from that point on.

In fact, I was fairly certain that Dr. Simons must have started his move out here, to the American Redoubt, shortly after that rather unfortunate quote and media firestorm. He'd stepped down as the chairman of the board of his company, Medical Frontiers, Inc., and had dropped out of the public eye. He re-emerged quietly as the director of the Fortress several years later.

None of it made sense to me, and I wanted to know why. From what I'd read about the Fortress in the handful of mainstream news articles describing its potential mission, it was a type of "last stand" for white, Christian fundamentalists who wanted nothing more to do with the ways of the big cities in the United States.

Dr. Simons, from what I'd read in the secular press accounts, had never much liked the Christian church and wanted little to do with it. Yet here he was, seemingly surrounded by what had been portrayed as a safe haven for those very same people who'd once condemned him as a gene-altering, species-corrupting monster.

And standing here in the public square, looking up at the new, all-brick buildings that ringed it, I could clearly see that this place was hardly some backwater village where barely literate zealots brought their belongings in the back of a pickup truck to camp out. There was money here—and a lot of it.

I turned my gaze back to Dr. Simons. "I have so many questions, I'm not even sure where to begin ..."

"How about the beginning?" he prompted. "That's always a good place to start, don't you think?"

"Sure, why not." I waved my right hand skyward as if swatting away some invisible insect that had been bothering me.

"Mind if we walk while we talk?" he asked. "My back doesn't hold up well these days if I sit for any length of time. Much better if I can stand and even better when I'm able to stroll along."

"Please. By all means. It'll give me a chance to see a bit of the place for myself."

Dr. Simons began to walk slowly away from the park bench. I could see that walking was difficult. I knew he was in his eighties now.

"You know, this place saved me," he said as we began to exit the public square onto a brick-and-cobblestone street that led upward, ever so gently, past small street-level shops of one kind or another and apartments with large windows. People smiled and nodded hello as we passed by. No one seemed in a hurry as they came in and out of the small shops along this particular street. "After that ..." He paused. I could see that the memory still pained him.

"The 'playing God' incident?" I offered.

"Yes, *that*. Everyone got it wrong. I never intended to say that I was trying to play God or even create a new species that was somehow better or different than the human species. That wasn't it at all. It was just a careless mistake told to a troublesome reporter I'd grown tired of talking to." He stopped, then looked at me. "Ah, sorry. I forget. You're a reporter too. I meant no direct slur to your profession."

"No worries, Dr. Simons. I'm not easily offended. And I'll do my best not to become troublesome."

He laughed. "Quite all right even if you do prove to be so. I'm beyond caring about such things or even what the world seems to think of me."

We walked a bit in silence. Dr. Simons let me soak in the ambiance of the place. It had a quiet, secure feel about it, reminding me of an academic setting. It invoked peacefulness and the urge to ask profound questions.

It was becoming obvious to me, as I walked along, that this place wasn't what it seemed to the outside world. We turned into yet another public square at the interior of the complex. Tables and benches and common areas were sprinkled throughout. Dozens of children clambered happily in and around structures at a playground tucked into a corner of this particular public square.

People were reading or typing or just chatting with each other in small groups. They all seemed content. What's more—and this took me quite by surprise—they were also not all white. Far from it, in fact. From my limited perspective, I could see that virtually every ethnicity was fully immersed in this community. There were no exclusions.

"This isn't really a fortress, is it?" I asked him finally.

He stopped and looked out over this interior public square. "Not in a military sense, if that's what you mean."

"So what is it then? And why did you call it *Fortress?*"

Dr. Simons stopped and gazed at the throngs of people taking part in community activities. "As I was saying, this place saved me. Or, rather, I should say: the people that you see here, these people here in this square, *they* saved me. When I left Medical Frontiers, I wanted to get away, as far as I possibly could. I'd had enough. I wanted nothing more to do with the world, or with people for that matter. All I wished for, with all my heart, was to escape and get away …"

"Off the grid," I said.

"In a manner of speaking, yes. But I didn't think of it that way at the time. I only wanted a simpler life without the questions. I wanted a place where no one thought of me as that person, that monster— the one they compared to Josef Mengele. I wanted a retreat, a respite. That was really all I was seeking. I bought this land on the side of this mountain, built a self-sufficient home, and prepared to let the world take its own course without me. And that's when I discovered a quite extraordinary thing."

"What?" I asked, genuinely curious now.

"They found me. I'd tried to hide. And I couldn't."

I shuddered. It was an instinctual thing, something I couldn't truly control. I fervently hoped that he wasn't referring to the same sorts of forces that Jude had always called on in our lives. "Who found you, Dr. Simons?" I asked, not entirely certain I wanted to hear the answer.

He swept his hand in front of him in a grand gesture. "Why, all of *them*. The people you see here. They came here for a freedom that they hadn't known, feared was being lost, and wished to rediscover. They wanted a place where they could engage in scientific, intellectual, philosophical, and religious pursuits with abandon and freedom. They didn't want rules and borders and laws and shackles. They wanted an open-source society, so to speak, where self-correcting actions and tasks kept the community moving forward, progressing."

"Toward what, Dr. Simons?"

"Who knows?" He shrugged. "And quite honestly, who cares? That's the beauty of open-source software—the community itself writes and rewrites the language to handle a nearly infinite number of tasks. And an open-source community or society functions nearly the same way. Given a certain freedom to try new things in an open and welcoming environment, I've learned from the people here that they will, in fact, not judge me or anyone else, but work to solve problems and move things forward in and around barriers and hurdles."

"So all of these people here …?"

"Came here for the ability to literally think without borders," Dr. Simons said. "It's an extraordinarily safe place for intellectual or scientific pursuit—in ways that even academia is no longer capable of due to political correctness and dogma. It is an open-source society, where each is free to contribute to the work of others."

"I can see this," I said slowly. "People say that they get the same sort of feeling when they walk around the Googleplex in California."

"There are some parallels, of course—more than you know. But they are a for-profit company. We are anything but, as you'll see."

"And the name—the Fortress?"

"From something entirely different than what you might think," Dr. Simons said with a twinkle in his eye. "It was merely a happy circumstance that the name, Fortress, also conveys a menacing, ominous perspective. Fortresses of old kept attackers out and protected those within. But that isn't where the name first came from. Follow me. I'll show you."

Dr. Simons started walking again. We turned down two side streets and came to a rather innocuous building with two simple doors as an entrance. The doors were unlocked. We walked in. "Welcome to Fortress," Dr. Simons said.

Inside were rows upon rows upon rows of parallel-processing machines, all humming and whirring with a quiet efficiency. A bearded man, perhaps in his late thirties, in jeans, Converse shoes, and a T-shirt, met us at the door as we entered. He extended his hand. "Lee Gentry," he said, shaking my hand vigorously. "I was the second resident here, thanks to Dr. Simon's invitation."

"What *is* this place?" I asked, trying to grasp the significance of what I was seeing.

"It's my home, in a manner of speaking, as well as our collective creation," Gentry said proudly.

"So what does that mean—'our creation'?" I asked.

"This," Gentry said, gesturing toward the rows of processors, "houses the greatest parallel-programming language on the planet, a tenth-generation successor to an open-source platform that was, once upon a time, built at Sun Microsystems to replace the Fortran computer language IBM built more than fifty years ago for the highest, most sophisticated computing needs in the world."

I regarded the rows of processors with newfound respect. "This … is a computer-programming language?"

"Not just any computing-programming language," Gentry explained. "It's a successor to Fortress, which Sun Microsystems once gave to the world as an open-source platform. It was built as a parallel-programming language, not dissimilar to the same sort of platform that Google uses to comb through the entire web on a daily basis for relevant, searchable information."

"So this is similar to something that Google uses?" I asked.

"Yes and no," Gentry clarified. "Fortress was designed to talk across multicore processors, not just from a single mainframe. Now this successor, which was built upon the original open-source platform, pulls power from literally millions of multicore processors—from all around the planet—in order to run programs."

"So you created Fortress for Sun Microsystems," I said, "and brought it here with you when it went open source and you became the second resident here?"

"Oh, good heavens, no!" Gentry said, laughing. "I didn't create Fortress. I wouldn't know the first thing about writing a computer-programming language, even BASIC. I'm a mechanical engineer. I put these processors together to run it."

"So who built it and brought it here?" I asked.

"I did," a sultry voice said from a few feet behind us.

All three of us turned. An elegant, attractive woman, clearly of Chinese descent, in a flowing summer dress and simple sandals practically glided across the floor from a windowless office that I hadn't noticed as we'd entered. I was mesmerized by her considerable beauty—something she'd probably had to deal with all her life.

"Yes," Gentry said. "Meet my wife, Kayla. She created Fortress and brought it here. I'm just the mechanic. Kayla is the creator."

"And you must be the enigmatic twin of Jude Asher, former chairman of the Federal Reserve, soon to be Senator Asher and president-in-waiting in just a matter of days," Kayla said, with a slight nod. I couldn't tell if she was serious or not. "We're honored to see you here."

I looked back at Dr. Simons. "So that's where the name of this place came from, then? This place is named after a new programming language built to run supercomputers?"

"Exactly," he said. "But since that early time, as many very talented and intellectually curious programmers have joined us and worked away at it—adding new and surprising complexity to it—we now have something vastly different than the original Fortress open-source programming language that Kayla once created and that both of them assembled here."

"So what is it now?"

"Well, not to put too fine a point on it—and at the risk of bringing back the old ghosts that once haunted me—I would say that this is now as close an approximation to the mind of God that you're likely to find on earth," he answered.

# CHAPTER TWENTY-FOUR

Jude and I had begun to drift in opposite directions even before he became chairman of the Federal Reserve following his dramatic efforts to yet again risk everything in order to short the Chinese yuan and keep the dollar from crashing.

The flattering profile in *Forbes* with the ridiculous and essentially unanswerable question—"Can He Save Us?"—hadn't made matters any better for us. I knew Jude. And I could safely say that no other human being on the planet did.

He was well on his way to a position where he could literally dictate the wealth of nations. I was still wondering why I was on the earth in the first place and about the meaning and frailty of human life. Jude had no time for such introspection. It was all I seemed to think about. He knew his own destiny.

More and more, I found myself wondering if Jude's master plan was worth it. As he gained control of pieces and places of the earth, I wondered about the cost—not to his soul, if such a thing existed, but simply to his humanity. He was becoming something other than a mere mortal with each passing day and new victory.

The forces that Jude had called on since our childhood didn't particularly bother me. I'd made peace in my own mind with the reality of Singen Prithar, the regents, and the others—*those things*—quite some time ago. They were lords of the world, pure and simple. If your aim was to master the earth, control it, bend it to your will, and subdue both peoples and nation-states for whatever purpose, then they were instruments of that war. They were necessary soldiers, from the captains and lieutenants to the foot soldiers. Jude had called on them for those purposes, and they obeyed.

Genghis Khan was thought to have killed 40 million people in his efforts to conquer the world. In the modern era, both Adolf Hitler and Joseph Stalin had been responsible for the deaths of millions in their respective quests to tame and control great portions of the earth. Their aims had been to gain the world at whatever cost. In all cases, they used whatever means and methods they had at hand to achieve their military and political ends. History judged them as cruel, wanton killers. But history could not erase their ability to conquer. In that, they had been wildly successful—for a time—by simply ignoring the conventional laws of morality.

I had no feeling, one way or the other, about Jude's morality. I know that should have troubled me. I'm sorry that it did not. Perhaps it was because he was my twin, and I could not condemn him. Perhaps it was because I'd only ever seen him call on forces to achieve specific, personal goals—not attempt to destroy people or nations. Perhaps I was just naive and blind.

I didn't view Jude as particularly evil or even all that manipulative. He was just extraordinarily skilled at getting what he wanted by any means necessary. He was a walking, living, breathing embodiment of the concept that the ends do justify the means. By that standard, Jude was successful in his efforts to master the universe. The world did, seemingly, belong to him.

Following his dramatic and quite successful move to keep the dollar from crashing, Jude had been compelled to accept the job as chairman of the Federal Reserve. The president's chief of staff had called Jude to the White House so he could be offered the position. He was thirty-five when he was appointed and confirmed by the US

Senate, making him the youngest Fed chairman ever—by a country mile.

Jude didn't even bother to ask me whether I'd agree to take over Asher Enterprises while he served as chairman of the Federal Reserve. He knew I'd never agree to work with Singen and the regents. I didn't even need to have that conversation with him. He placed our assets in a blind trust, with Singen as caretaker, while he took control of the largest private banking system in the history of the world.

In truth, Jude rarely asked for my counsel or advice on anything any longer. He didn't require it for Asher Enterprises—he'd had my proxy for as long as either of us could remember. There was virtually no piece of advice I could offer that outranked what he received from his regents, counselors, and advisors. He no longer needed either a sidekick or a validator for his actions. He had an adoring public for that now.

Now when he called me, it seemed like a summons. Which is precisely what it felt like the day he phoned to see if I could join him in Washington later that week to meet someone. He'd called me from aboard Air Force One as he was accompanying the president to the G8 Summit in Brussels. I was certain he'd gone out of his way to phone me from the president's plane just to annoy me.

"Why are you calling?" I asked wearily. "And did you *really* have to call me from Air Force One? It couldn't have waited until you'd landed in Europe?"

"This is a lot more fun," Jude said. "Admit it."

"I won't admit anything. So why'd you call?"

"To make sure you can meet someone."

"Who?" Jude had stopped going to red-carpet events with Hollywood actresses and Ford models. In fact, I hadn't seen a picture

of him in the tabloids in ages. That, alone, should have told me
something had changed.

"You'll see," he said mysteriously. "You'll like her. She has an
exotic name and an even more exotic background. Plus, she's beautiful, and she might be a princess because of the family she was adopted
into ..."

"Wait," I said. "She's an orphan?'

"Yes. Like us. And she may be the one."

"The one what?" I asked, a bit incredulous. It had never occurred
to me that Jude would ever settle down. "Like the person you're
going to marry some day?"

"Yes, maybe. I don't know. We just met at a state dinner in Paris.
We visited the Louvre the next day. She knew every artist, every story
behind nearly every painting we came across. She is a tour de force."

"So she's into art?"

"Not just art. She seems to know something about nearly
everything—politics, art, culture, history, even sports. She knew the
story and history behind Alydar's Ghost, for crying out loud!"

"Half the world knows the backstory of Alydar's Ghost and the
Triple Crown, thanks to you and your big mouth," I chided him
gently.

"Yeah, well, she knew the last five teams to win the Super Bowl,
the World Series, and even the Stanley Cup. I don't know those,
and I'll bet you don't, either. I had to look them up just to see—and
she was right. And then, for good measure, at dinner last night, she
rattled off the names of every world leader in two dozen countries
on all six continents. I'd asked her to name one or two, merely as a
joke, and I had to stop her before she went through the entire list of
countries on the planet."

"So, what, she has a photographic memory?"

"Beats me. All I know is that she's both the smartest—and most beautiful—woman I've ever met."

I whistled softly. "That's saying something, Jude. You aren't easily impressed."

"So you'll meet her? See what you think?"

"You need my blessing for something like this? Since when?"

"Since you're the only family I have, which you somehow keep managing to forget. We'll be in DC for a state dinner at the White House. I can get you two tickets at the president's table. Can I count on you?"

I closed my eyes. It really did feel like a summons. "Sure, why not? I'll come meet your mystery princess, if you insist. But I can't promise I'll bring a date."

"Don't worry. Just be there. And remember, it's black tie. You can't show up in your usual slacker suit."

It was pathetic, actually. Because I was sitting at the head table with the president and the first lady—not to mention the chairman of the Federal Reserve and his special guest—I had to endure not one, but three successive, meaningless conversations as I ran the gauntlet just to get to the first course of the meal.

It turned out that there is an elaborate and quite strict protocol for state dinners at the White House. Who knew?

First, I spoke to the White House social secretary. I quickly concluded that she had a thoroughly thankless job—all risk and very little reward. If she made a mistake, she was toast. And success was measured simply by the lack of mistakes. Then there was the White House chief usher. In past eras, this person might properly have been the lead servant. Now they had a fancier title. I didn't envy this person his job, which seemed primarily to consist of making sure the food was served as unobtrusively as possible. And finally, there was the chief of protocol of the United States, who worked at the State Department. I had no idea what this person did, other than to make sure weird diplomatic gaffes didn't occur. This, too, seemed like a particularly thankless job.

I hadn't even bothered to find out who this particular White House state dinner was honoring. Honestly, I didn't care. I'd flown to DC on the shuttle from New York simply because I'd been summoned by Jude. It turned out that it was kind of a big deal as state dinners go. The king of Norway was in town. I wasn't entirely sure how many kings and queens were left in various parts of the world. But surely there weren't many of them left, so this had to be a bit special as these things went.

When I finally cleared the diplomatic gauntlet and entered the actual State Dining Room, I scanned the room of elaborate, round tables to see if I could find my brother. When I finally saw him—standing next to the president—I knew instantly why I was here.

I'd been to more red-carpet and eye-candy social events with Jude than I wanted to count since we'd inherited our fortune from the Ashers. I'd been to world premieres with the best-known actresses in Hollywood. I'd consorted with supermodels on immaculate beaches beneath sun-kissed villas in various parts of the world. I'd sat in owners' boxes at Super Bowls and world championships with tall, tanned, and perfectly manicured women who'd won Miss Universe titles.

None of them compared to the woman standing beside Jude across the room.

Every single eye in the room—male and female—was stealing glances in her direction. Some did it unashamedly. Others did it furtively. But all tried, at some point, to look at the woman in the shimmering gold, floor-length dress with its modest neckline.

It was nearly impossible to discern her ethnicity or what part of the world she hailed from. The dark brown features of her face were framed by smooth, shoulder-length black hair.

As I made my way through the crowded room toward the head table, she turned her long neck in my direction. Her hair swept away from her face. Our eyes met. I could see the immediate recognition in her visage. She smiled at me. Despite my best intentions, I smiled back and did my best to still my heart.

She separated herself as I approached the head table. She took three graceful steps away from the president's party that was gathered, standing, beside the table and intercepted me before I could reach my brother and the others. She extended her left hand toward me, palm down. Again, despite my best intention, I took it. She squeezed it affectionately, as if we'd been friends for years.

"Thomas, I am *so* happy that you agreed to join us," she said. "I've so looked forward to this moment and our time together this evening."

I was slightly disoriented for a moment. Her beauty was magnified at such close range, making it difficult to think clearly.

Jude looked over at that moment, caught sight of the two of us talking, and tilted his head to one side. His unspoken question to me was obvious.

"I … I'm sorry," I stuttered. "I would introduce myself to you properly, but my brother didn't tell me your name when he invited me to this dinner."

She turned away quickly, casting a disapproving glance back at Jude. As she looked away, I noticed the stunning diamond necklace she wore—a small figurine with two slim arms hanging to the side. It was not dissimilar to an ankh and was attached to a slim, gold chain. I'd seen something like it before, though I couldn't place it exactly. It was attractive and distinctive. It stood for something.

"How rude of your brother," she said, pivoting fluidly back toward me. Despite my efforts to ignore others around us, I could see that quite a few onlookers continued to steal glances in our direction. "He shouldn't have done that to you." She extended her right hand more formally this time. "My name is Isis Kent, and I am thoroughly delighted to make your acquaintance."

I tried not to stare. I held onto her right hand far longer than I should have. "I am … delighted to meet you as well," I finally managed.

She took a step closer. "Don't worry," she said to me in a hushed half whisper. "People have that sort of reaction all the time. I know it's an unusual name. But it was the one they gave me when I was adopted in New Zealand. I like it actually, and I do enjoy the looks I get when I first introduce myself."

"I'm so sorry," I offered. "I'm not usually so inarticulate. But I believe Jude basically set me up here. He told me virtually nothing about you—where you're from, what you do for a living, even your name. I know nothing about you whatsoever, and I'll wager you know a great deal about me already thanks to Jude."

"Yes, it's not fair," she said with a light laugh. "So we must balance the equation a bit here, I believe. I will tell you more about myself. But in return, you must agree to tell me some things about your brother that I don't already know. Deal?"

"It's a deal," I said with a sigh, thankful that my social ineptness was apparent only to her—and that she had clearly already forgiven me.

We spent the balance of the state dinner talking, she and I. Jude left us alone—either by design or accident. He spent most of his time networking. He made a point of visiting every table at the dinner, which left Isis and me to talk quietly. I was a bit surprised at her choice. She actually ignored the world's most powerful leader, seated two chairs away, to focus on her conversation with me.

Isis wasn't her original birth name, she told me. She'd been born in Egypt, and whatever records existed of her birth were lost. She'd spent years searching records in Cairo, trying to find her original birth parents, with no luck. For whatever reason, she'd been orphaned during a period of civil unrest in Egypt. A New Zealand couple, diplomats, had adopted her when she was nearly a year old, she said.

It was only years later, she said, when she was a teenager, that she'd learned the history of the Kents, the couple who had adopted her. The Kents were distant cousins in the House of Windsor, long transplanted halfway around the world to the untamed coast of New Zealand.

"So you're royalty?" I asked her.

"Hardly," she said, raising a well-manicured brow. "I'm an orphan rug rat."

"But you were adopted into the ... the what? The House of Kent?"

She laughed at that. "If by 'the house of Kent' you mean the farm cottage on the coast of New Zealand where I grew up and looked after the sheep to make sure they didn't run off the cliff into the ocean, then, yes."

"But you're connected to the House of Windsor?"

"In as roundabout way as you could possibly imagine. I've never actually met any of my cousins, and I seriously doubt anyone in the House of Windsor has ever heard of the Kents of New Zealand."

"Really? Never?"

"The closest I will likely ever come to the royal House of Windsor is the time I spent as a Rhodes Scholar at Oxford."

"So you were a Rhodes Scholar?" I said in awe.

"Sure, after graduating from St. Andrews."

"The University of St. Andrews in Scotland?" I grew more impressed with Isis's mind with each turn of our conversation. "That's one of the finest universities in the world."

"Not if you ask anyone from Cambridge or Oxford," she said dryly.

That made *me* laugh. Jude went to Harvard. I went to Duke. I liked this woman.

"So why'd the Kents name you Isis?" I finally managed to ask her at some point in our conversation.

"They wouldn't tell me. But I suspect it was a private joke between the two of them at first. And then the name stuck. They never actually got around to telling me why. It's just the name I grew up with. And now I can't ask them …"

"So they're both dead?" I asked gently.

"They were caught in a bloody uprising while he was stationed in the Congo. They were both killed before they could get out of the country."

"I'm sorry," I offered.

"Thank you. But it was years ago. I've been on my own for some time now."

She'd been all over the world in the past ten years, to some of the most troubled spots on the planet, and now spoke at least six languages fluently. She'd gone with the United Nations as part of a peacekeeping mission to southern Lebanon where she'd been able to spend time with the leadership of the Hezbollah. She'd spent time in Pakistan, Yemen, and Sudan. She'd even been on a charity food mission to North Korea before they'd ended such outside missions. She seemed fearless.

By the end of the evening, I fully understood why Jude was so taken with her. Isis was perfect in every conceivable way. There seemed to be virtually no flaw in her. She was even diplomatic about her religious beliefs. The Kents had been Christians; Isis had managed to befriend Shi'a and Sunni alike in Lebanon; and she spoke knowledgeably and passionately about her study of Brahman—the "unchanging, highest reality" she hoped might someday explain her own human nature in a physical, material world. She'd taken the parts of each world religion that most appealed to her, she said, and jettisoned the parts that fueled hate and paranoia. It was an answer worthy of a self-effacing religious leader.

"Didn't I tell you?" Jude asked me as we were leaving the White House amidst the camera flashes of news photographers taking pictures of the guests.

"You did," I said approvingly. "She's extraordinary. I'm in awe. I feel like I've known her for years."

"So she's a keeper?" he asked. Then he winked and entered a black limousine.

"Yes, I'd say so," I said.

The door closed, and the limousine pulled away. I was suddenly a bit saddened and depressed that the evening had ended.

# Chapter Twenty-Five

"Go ahead. Try it."

Kayla was insistent and not the least bit defensive about her creation. She had considerable faith in its abilities.

Or rather, the abilities of the community it commanded and drew from. For that, as she explained, was the beauty of Fortress.

"It is capable of critical evaluation and randomized assessment in a neural network environment," she said.

"You do realize," I said slowly, as I stared out over the rows of what seemed like nothing more than a very large stack of individual computers, "that I have no idea at all what any of that means. It's Martian to me."

"Martian isn't a language," Kayla tossed back.

"My point exactly." I smiled. "You could explain how a language can make inanimate objects do things, and it might as well be Martian to me. It's completely foreign. I have no hope of understanding it. I nearly failed calculus in high school."

I glanced over at Dr. Simons and Kayla's husband, who were clearly enjoying themselves. I wondered whether either of them understood what Kayla was trying to explain to me—or whether they were just really good at faking it.

Kayla's expressive brows crinkled for a minute in thought. "Okay, let me try this. Once upon a time, there was a big, round machine called the Cray-1. It was built for Los Alamos Lab in the 1970s and was mostly a series of wedges and gates stitched and linked together to process millions of lines of individual instructions—or code—to achieve certain results. It was the first of what came to be known as supercomputers—really big computers that could run lots of stuff at high speeds. The boxes just kept getting bigger and bigger. At one point, one of these supercomputers could take up an entire floor of a building.

"But then a curious thing happened. Other companies, like Google, came along and learned how to run those millions of lines of instructions across lots and lots of processors running in parallel. Software programmers at Google and elsewhere learned how to do parallel programming across all of these linked but separate pieces. We even started to learn how to separate out what was inconsequential and to isolate what we needed to pay close attention to or what was truly meaningful to any given task. That's where things started to get very interesting, as far as I was concerned.

"Because that's actually the way our brains work. Each of us literally walk around with a giant supercomputer hardwired to physical things, such as our body and its ability to sense smell and texture, or our eyes, which can detect color and motion. We are able to process both trivial and meaningful stimuli at the same time and arrive at meaningful conclusions. Our brains can literally separate the wheat from the chaff.

"For instance, when we see something, our brain separates out all of the different physical characteristics and then compares them against our own stored memories—in the brain's hard drive, so to speak—and decides what's important. Our concept of beauty, for instance, is a combination of what we see in the present compared against a value we've assigned to our stored memories. Beauty, in this case, is literally in the eye of the beholder—but only as our brain performs parallel processing to arrive at such a designation.

"Parallel processing in computers—and the ability to write a language like Fortress to take advantage of it—follows generally along the same sort of track. People have been trying to mirror the brain's ability to process things in parallel for decades—without a whole lot of success. The basic problem is that it's like trying to use the collective consciousness of a whole bunch of brains all at the same time—and each brain has its own will and gets in the way of the collective task.

"Fortress and others tried to solve this dilemma by creating really sophisticated software—which you can think of as a language with instructions—that distributes the words of that language across everything in such a way that it doesn't put too much stress on any single core, or brain. It's the only way in which parallel programming across many, many cores could ever work.

"Not even Google, as powerful as it is, has been able to replicate the nearly magical way in which a single, individual brain is able to take in random information, process it, and then create rational thought. Not really. It can make guesses at rational thought. And parallel processing can produce some pretty extraordinary guesses that show up in your search box for instance.

"But it isn't actually *thinking*. Not in the way that you and I imagine rational thought from a brain. It's why artificial intelligence has failed over and over. We haven't been able to program anything to take illogical, irrational, seemingly inconsequential bits of data and information in a constant, unstructured stream and produce something beautiful or meaningful from it the way a brain does. We just haven't, not in years of trying.

"Until now. Until Fortress. What we have here—at least, the Fortress here, now, in its tenth generation—is the synthesis of many millions of brains all essentially agreeing to put their own selfishness aside for the tasks we assign it. It wasn't easy. We've had the best software programmers from MIT, Caltech, Stanford, and elsewhere roll through here to try their hands at things in this open-source environment. There was constant, endless failure. I mean, catastrophic and dismal failure. Dead end after dead end.

"The breakthrough occurred when everyone stopped trying so hard on their own to solve the grand equation that mimics the human brain. That was when—if I can use so inelegant and inexact a phrase—'the magic happened.' It was only when everyone stopped trying to think individually that Fortress actually started to work as some of us had hoped. Someone would write a bit of something, randomly, that seemed to make no sense. Then they'd quit. Someone else would pick it up—as if it were a random lyric from a distantly familiar song—and add to it. Then someone else would pick up that thread, add to it, and pass it along. It was only then that we were able to finally begin to collectively write parallel-programming language capable of taking over and running through many cores and pulling out the meaningful bits.

"The secret, we finally learned, was that the process had to be both intuitive and interactive, because that's the way our minds and brains work. In effect, it had to be a two-way street—or many, many streets all at the same time. It had to be a community approach to processing information—not a linear or singular approach.

"It was then that Fortress grew up and became like us."

As Kayla talked, she'd grown more and more animated. I could see, clearly, that whatever this was in front of us was her life's work. I still had no real idea what Fortress was. But I could tell, from the snippets I'd put together of her words, what it might represent.

I could also see that both Dr. Simons and Kayla's husband were extraordinarily proud of what she'd been able to accomplish—whether they understood it or not.

"How is this approach different from what Google's search engine is capable of?" I asked. "And, if I may be so rude, why is the Fortress—the physical place I've arrived at here built on the side of this mountain—any different than the Googleplex that prides itself on its ability to let geniuses tinker in their spare time one day a week and come up with mind-bending, planet-altering solutions?"

Dr. Simons started chuckling. "I'll let Kayla answer the first part. But let me ask you a question first."

"Fire away," I said.

"Have you ever actually been to the Googleplex?" he asked.

I paused. "No, I haven't."

"Well, if you had," Dr. Simons said, "they'd have asked you to sign a piece of paper as you walked inside that, in essence, says that anything you dream up or think about while you're there belongs to them, to Google. In effect, your thoughts aren't really yours—they belong to Google. And as for the ability to go off and think big thoughts a day a week, that's all well and good. But, as we've learned here, it takes much, much more than that. It requires immersion in a community of like-minded others all willing to share their unconnected thoughts, solutions, and ideas on a constant basis without any thought of whether it was intellectual property or not. A 'world without end' intellectual approach."

"And to answer the first part of your question," Kayla said, "Fortress isn't search. Not even close. Search—whether it's Google or Bing or anything else—takes a question and gives you the best, most appropriate, most relevant answer to your question. It searches through literally everything on the web and then ranks answers to your question in the order that algorithms predict are most helpful and useful to you, the person who asked the initial question. Different algorithms produce different answers.

"Fortress will ultimately give you answers to the question you didn't ask but meant to. It *interprets* what you've asked and tries to produce better answers to your question. Let's say that you type the word *apple* into a Google search engine. There's a pretty good chance that what you get back first will be the website for the company, followed immediately by the latest news articles mentioning the company. Eventually, if you keep paging through the results, you'll come to a website or page that describes an actual apple, its nutritional value, or the history and meaning behind the theory that eating an apple a day is good for you.

"But if you ask the same question of Fortress, you'll see a vastly different response and a much different process. It will be a two-way street. It will be interactive and intuitive. Fortress will actually try to learn from you, and then reach out to other cores that have the best ability to process that information."

I held up my hand. "Wait a minute. You mean it will ask me questions?"

"Exactly," Kayla said. "Like a doctor sitting with a patient who asks questions from a number of different directions until she is able to offer up a diagnosis—one that is based on both book knowledge and learning. That diagnosis closely correlates to what she intuitively believes is the likely cause of the malady."

"So I should call it *Doctor* Fortress?" I joked.

"You could," Kayla replied, "and you wouldn't be too far off the mark."

I looked back at the softly whirring batch of processors in front of me with newfound admiration. "So all of that is stored right here, in this room? Fortress manages that right here?"

"Actually, no," Kayla explained. "What you see here is just the portal into the only true way in which any of this is possible. It's a gateway to one big, global networking community. The true power is out there in the community of hundreds of millions of computers. That's why it's called parallel processing—it allows lots of things to happen out there, in a community, literally all at the same time.

"While we, the human species, didn't specifically set out to build one giant, supercomputing brain, that's essentially what we did with the World Wide Web and its vast stores of compartmentalized data and information. What Fortress has done is allow that brain to think for itself by asking questions instead of simply responding to what humans ask of it.

"So just as God, should He exist, would interact with us to see what we truly want in life—and not just tell us what to do under a predefined set of rules and algorithms—Fortress seeks out what we are truly asking for when we interact with it. And then it answers us in kind."

# Chapter Twenty-Six

It had been Singen's idea. At least, that was what Jude told me. But who knew, really? As time passed, I was having a more difficult time distinguishing between Singen's suggestions and Jude's decisions. I had to admit, though, it was a master stroke. Isis thought so as well.

Jude had grown bored with his job as chairman of the Federal Reserve almost immediately. I could hear it in his voice the first time he had to testify in front of the Senate Finance Committee and actually talk about quantitative easing.

Seriously, hearing Jude testify about the last resort of the central banking system when nothing else was working to stimulate the US economy was like listening to screeching fingernails on a blackboard—to me, at least.

Jude had kept the dollar from crashing, but the American economy still hadn't really recovered. And it wasn't like China would roll over and play dead. No, the Chinese leadership kept an even tighter rein on their own currency after Jude had manipulated the global currency markets.

The Chinese had redoubled their efforts to protect their export markets—and, thereby their own economy—and there wasn't much Jude or anyone else could do about it. The Chinese weren't about to be sucker punched a second time on their currency.

Which left Jude and the other central banks little choice. The Federal Reserve had lowered their target interest rates to *below* zero, and it still hadn't revived a moribund economy. So Jude was left with quantitative easing, where the Fed increases the monetary base by purchasing financial assets from commercial banks.

Yet I could tell, listening to him, his heart wasn't in it. It wasn't that he didn't care intellectually or that he wasn't at least somewhat interested in reviving the economy. It was mostly that there was very little challenge in the effort. The banking system moved at a glacial pace. Jude was far more interested in taking enormous risks and moving at the speed of light. It was a mismatch.

The Fed seemed to agonize over decisions about whether to move the target interest rate up or down by a quarter of a percent. Jude, I knew, could not have cared less one way or the other. And it came through in his interviews to the press. Which is why Singen's idea, seconded by Isis, was so thoroughly brilliant. It gave Jude something to talk about again—something that quickened his pulse. And if it worked, it would have the added benefit of jump-starting the American economy again.

The gap between the Haves and the Have-Nots in America and other developed countries had grown to profoundly ludicrous proportions. And despite efforts by Washington to level the playing field through tax reform, the gap between the rich and the poor grew wider every year.

There were more billionaires in America than at any time in history. Yet at the same time, the number of people on food stamps had doubled in less than a decade to nearly 50 million people. One in three people in America were on food stamps, now known as the Supplemental Nutrition Assistance Program. And the actual amount of money that Washington needed to spend to keep that 50 million fed through SNAP had tripled in the same time period.

The disparity was obscene, and everyone knew it. Years earlier, a movement had begun among some of the very wealthiest in America that was called the Giving Pledge. It began with Bill Gates and

Warren Buffett, who both pledged to give at least half of their wealth to philanthropic causes. Within three years, more than 100 billionaires had signed up and pledged to give at least half of their fortunes to charity. Those pledges alone meant that nearly $200 billion was being pledged to charity or philanthropic organizations. Even that, however, was a fraction of the actual wealth controlled by individual billionaires and their families.

In fact, the Giving Pledge represented less than 10 percent of the number of individual billionaires in the world now, and that didn't even count the families or government dictators who controlled vast wealth. In all, the hundred or so billionaires who'd signed up for the Giving Pledge represented probably 1 or 2 percent of the wealth that had consolidated in the hands of several thousand people on the planet. The thousand or so individual billionaires on the planet controlled more than $5 trillion alone just by themselves.

When family fortunes, wealthy dictators, and royal families were thrown in to the mix, a relatively small number of people—no more than a few thousand on a planet of seven billion—now controlled two-thirds of all the wealth on earth. A new empire of rulers—the scions of wealth—now loosely controlled a confederacy of economic activity on an unprecedented, global scale.

Still, the Giving Pledge was a high-minded approach to philanthropy, and certainly better than simply waiting until you died and bequeathing your estate so a new building could be named after you on a college campus. It was a moral commitment, not a legal or binding contract. Jude and I had considered the Giving Pledge for years, in fact, and had gone back and forth about the utility of it.

Curiously, though, the list of billionaires who refused to entertain the notion of the Giving Pledge was nearly as interesting as the list of more than 100 billionaires who had agreed to it. Some opposed it on their own moral grounds—they preferred to control their assets even beyond the grave, if necessary. Still others opposed it purely on the principle that they'd worked hard to build up their wealth and had no intention of simply giving it away to others who had no idea how to spend it. And there were a few, of course, who simply didn't care—about philanthropy, doing good, or even creating a decent public image for themselves through charitable efforts.

The organizers of the Giving Pledge held secret meetings in cities such as New York and Paris to recruit other billionaires into the campaign. Singen and Jude went to one of these meetings, and the idea was born there.

"What about a *Spending* Pledge?" Jude had asked me shortly after he and Singen had returned from this secret meeting.

"A what?" I said, distracted.

I had recently taken my job at *The New York Times*, and it had been a very long day. Jude had called me almost immediately after his plane had landed at JFK. We met at the entrance to Central Park South and were now walking along the east side of the park as the sun set behind the buildings on the west.

"A pledge by these billionaires to pool their money, not just give it away," he said as we walked along. I could tell Jude was excited by the idea. I hadn't heard enthusiasm in his voice about an idea like this in ages. "Isis thinks it's utterly brilliant, and that it might work. Singen is all for it as well."

"What do you mean—pool their money?" I asked. "How would that work, exactly?"

"Most of the people at this meeting I just came back from are ... well, constitutionally incapable of giving away their money to charity. It seems like a waste of hard-earned wealth to them. Nearly all have had miserable experiences with the nonprofit world—with the lack of strategic direction, the small-mindedness and aimlessness of it all. They're used to getting results, both with their wealth and with their businesses. Charity seems … pointless to them."

"I can understand that. It's one of the reasons I don't run around in the nonprofit world myself. I prefer working."

Jude laughed. He never would understand why I kept up the charade of writing for a living when I didn't have to. "So here's the idea. Why not ask people to spend their money, not just give it away? If the point is to do some good with it—to make a difference in the world—then they should do that. Do some good with it. Spend it on something rather than simply give it away."

It made sense. The Bill and Melinda Gates Foundation had operated a bit like that for years. It funded research, like a corporation, and developed vaccines. It wasn't really a charity—it ran more like a business, with goals like eradicating polio or malaria. It operated so much like a company that it had actually displaced some of the work done by other companies in the global public health space.

But virtually no other philanthropy operated like the Gates Foundation. No one had ever even tried … which is why Jude's idea wasn't totally insane.

"But how would it work, exactly?" I prodded. "I have a tough time seeing all of these folks working together. It isn't exactly in their nature or DNA to collaborate together on common goals. They're all pretty individualistic."

That's when I saw it—the fire in his eyes. Jude knew this was a big idea, the kind that could take the world by storm and shake it to its very foundation. And he wanted to be the person who did the shaking. Atlas may have shrugged once. Jude wanted to pick that world back up and carry it forward on his own shoulders.

"It will be a collection of individuals who can achieve more together than they ever could apart," he said. "Isis has already begun to put together the list of all the big ideas that just need capital behind them. Kids still die every three seconds from easily preventable diseases, for instance. So that goes right at the top of our list. We need a permanent renewable energy source that's cheaper than anything now available. We need a new way to grow food efficiently before we run out of arable land. A single billionaire couldn't possibly solve those equations alone—not even us. But together, across all of the different networks and industries that we'd be in a position to draw from if we pooled our wealth together as part of a Spending Pledge, that's a completely different story. A collection of individuals who control the world's wealth can achieve together what individuals alone have no hope of accomplishing apart."

It was an interesting concept—global economic development masquerading as philanthropy. Something only Jude could create.

"So … what, then? The funds are used to build enterprises, start new businesses that address unmet needs? That sort of thing?"

"Sure, why not? Every one of these billionaires is used to building things, creating things. It's why they're so uneasy about giving away their wealth. They'd be infinitely more comfortable using it to actually build and create things that solve big problems. Jobs would be created. Communities would be helped. Economies of scale would be achieved. A new, better, global financial empire would rise from the dustbin of global economic decay. And it wouldn't rely on individual charitable efforts. The power of the many, fueled by a vast network of wealth, would change everything."

My brother's eyes practically smoldered with excitement.

"And I'll bet you have a name for this already, don't you?" I said.

We both stepped to the side of the road as a horse and carriage clacked past us.

"Somehow the Spending Pledge doesn't quite work, I don't think," I said.

"I do have a name, or rather Isis came up with one," Jude replied. "We'll simply call it the Good Earth campaign. I can raise the profile for it just by talking about it with the media worldwide."

"While you're still running the Fed?"

"I could, I suppose." Jude shrugged. "It's just me talking. Who's going to stop me from doing that? It's what I'm good at, after all."

"But you're not going to do that, are you?"

I knew Jude better than anyone. I'd seen it in his eyes, heard it in his voice when he spoke about the world's monetary systems at public meetings. He'd had enough. He'd mastered the wealth of nations. He'd learned everything that he possibly could. There was no reason for him to remain as chairman of the Federal Reserve any longer.

"I'm going to resign from the Fed—next week, in fact," he said, his tone matter-of-fact. "I've already let the White House know. They weren't happy. I'll let the board of governors know later this week. They won't be pleased, either—at least, the ones with no interest in jockeying to succeed me."

"And pursue this campaign and nothing else?" I asked. Somehow, I doubted that was *all* Jude had on his mind.

"I believe we can raise a trillion dollars—or two or three trillion dollars—for the Good Earth campaign. It would be the largest, single collection of wealth dedicated to doing good for the planet—ever.

With that kind of money pledged, virtually nothing is beyond reach. Nothing at all."

Billionaire publisher Malcolm Forbes—who threw lavish parties on private yachts for movie stars like Elizabeth Taylor, and collected vast collections of art, antique model boats, toy soldiers, and ancient manuscripts—once famously said, "He who dies with the most toys wins." But Jude had outgrown any compulsive need to acquire toys and trinkets years earlier. He was now vastly more interested in other types of acquisitions. I also knew he had no interest in keeping score after he died. He was much more interested in keeping score while he was very much alive.

"But you have something else in mind, don't you?" I asked him. "Something you want to do before you get there?"

"I do. It's actually something I should have dealt with before now," Jude said mysteriously. "The Good Earth campaign will follow later, once I've gotten my house in order."

# Chapter Twenty-Seven

I could have stayed at Fortress forever. It was unlike anything I'd expected, and it took my breath away. Everywhere I walked with Kayla and Lee Gentry and Dr. Simons was a new wonder. I'd never seen or experienced anything like it in my life.

I knew, from firsthand experience, that there were very few places on earth where you could learn simply for the sake of learning—with no rules or governance or expectations. Research had goals and aims and milestones and final reports. Academia had rules and bureaucracy and systems. Think tanks faced the constant necessity of replenishing their source of funding. Fortress had none of these constraints, largely thanks to Dr. Simons's view of philanthropy.

What further delighted me was the rather unexpected and pleasant discovery that religious learning also knew no bounds whatsoever at Fortress. Yes, there were Christian believers and learners. But there were also Hindus, Buddhists, Jews, and Muslims. And they all talked to each other—regularly and politely.

"Fortress demands nothing," he told me, "except intellectual curiosity and a willingness to take risks without fear of failure. I've always been happy to maintain the overhead. I feel like it is the least I can do, given the riches that the world has bestowed on me in my lifetime. All you have to do is open your mind while you're here."

Plato's Academy must have been like this, once—a great learning center where critical thinking was encouraged simply for the sake of benefitting others in the community as opposed to creating intellectual property.

I'd been expecting hate, paranoia, isolation, and fear here at the center of the American Redoubt. What I found—at least in this one particular corner of the Redoubt—was a largely stress-free community of very smart professionals in a variety of technological fields who were committed to just one thing—interactive, open-source creation of software and hardware technology tools that advanced knowledge.

It turned out that Fortress was actually a place of retreat and respite in the narrowest of terms. People were invited to spend sabbaticals at Fortress. But once they were on campus, they could remain as long as they liked. Some had signed up for a year and had remained well beyond their sabbatical. Others took every opportunity to fly back and forth from Fortress when they could. Still others found ways to live and work from Fortress remotely. But all of them had one common goal—interactive knowledge creation with no restraints or borders.

Dr. Simons had built the core of Fortress, initially, as his home. When Kayla and Lee had shown up, they'd built a second residence alongside it. As others joined them, they continued to push the perimeter of Fortress outward.

Dr. Simons freely spent his own wealth to help those who needed it and freely built pieces of critical infrastructure necessary to support both the community of learning as well as the interconnected digital links to the rest of the world. Fortress was clearly going to be Dr. Simons's living legacy.

"But does any of it actually benefit people?" I asked Kayla on one of the many walks we took together through the campus. I learned something new on every walk. Part of the Fortress campus, for instance, was an open amphitheater where someone interesting gave a lecture every morning. Another part was a book corner under an awning where authors talked about works they'd created. Still another part of the campus was an effort to digitally recreate the library of great works that had once perished at Alexandria. And yet another part of the campus was an open gymnasium where some sort of game or contest was always underway. The list of possibilities appeared endless. There seemed to be no intellectual limits on campus.

"I mean, this is all well and good," I continued. "I've certainly enjoyed my stay here. It's a bit like an intellectual spa or academic resort. But the things that are created here, like Fortress itself—does it do any good? Is learning with no promise of immediate financial or personal reward actually good for anything?"

Kayla nodded. The question apparently wasn't a new one for her or the community of learners. "People have been debating the merits or drawbacks of open-source creation for years now," she said. "It's very difficult to make money or build businesses around open-source knowledge that is freely available to the world. At least, that's what they teach you in business school. And there's some truth to that.

"Fortress has taken that concept to its extreme—and tested the limits of its usefulness. And while we've all certainly taken some winding roads into one dead end or another, we've also learned something quite valuable—that a community dedicated to learning and growing without intellectual borders eventually sorts itself out into a process that creates something capable of achieving greatness.

"I can tell you that when I first started working on Fortress as a new language, I was obsessed with creating something that would build value for a company. That was my goal. I thought Fortress would replace the first computer language. I thought it would serve a very useful business function and make me wealthy in the process. But the company where I worked changed direction, and Fortress became irrelevant to its business mission. The language existed, but there was no one to speak it—until I came here.

"That's when everything changed for me. I discovered that there were others who wanted to speak the language with me and turn it into something that would, in fact, be useful. Fortress became a living, breathing thing then. And, yes, it became useful for people.

"Fortress, for instance, has spawned nearly one hundred new, incredibly powerful software and web companies in education, medical, and other fields. And we have literally dozens of other similar stories from the physical campus—people who come here, learn from the community, and then go back to the world from here armed with new knowledge that makes progress in commercial fields.

"But there is one simple reason I know that Fortress, all by itself, is now quite valuable. The National Security Agency has tried to acquire it from us now on at least five separate occasions. They've approached Dr. Simons three times, and me on two other occasions at high-end computing workshops in Palo Alto and Boston. We've tried to decline NSA's requests each time by explaining that it isn't really a discreet, standalone system—that it's more properly a living, growing, interactive computing language the Fortress programming community keeps adding to almost daily. NSA either doesn't believe that or refuses to.

"NSA seems to see something in Fortress that they are simply unable to buy, build, steal, or re-create, so they keep taking a run at us to acquire it for themselves. All of their needle-in-the-haystack data-mining systems built by Palantir and efforts like PRISM don't seem to compare to what Fortress is now capable of, apparently. I know that I'll keep saying no to their request, and I assume Dr. Simons will as well—if only because we don't actually own it. Fortress belongs to the community. So, yes, I would say that this sort of grand experiment in learning without borders is useful to people."

There was still one task I'd been reluctant to try from the moment I'd arrived, and I wasn't sure I wanted to try it even now. Kayla and Lee hadn't pressed me on it. But Dr. Simons had. He'd been insistent, in fact.

I hadn't actually asked Fortress a question—on any subject— that was useful or relevant to me personally. I'd watched Kayla give demonstrations on various subjects, from sports to business to pop culture. Lee and Dr. Simons had given demonstrations on its ability to create intuitive links to many interesting intellectual pursuits and conversations as well.

But none of it was relevant to me, personally. And I didn't know if I wanted to test myself—or what I knew—against Fortress.

I had never spoken of anything I knew about Jude to another soul on the planet. I'd never granted a single interview to a reporter. I'd never breathed a word of anything behind the scenes about the globe-trotting, game-changing, world-dominating Jude Asher who had taken his Good Earth campaign and created a vast, new, global financial empire that remade the world as we knew it almost overnight.

I'd also never voiced another of my secret suspicions to a soul, either. And I was, even now, a bit afraid of seeking an answer to this other secret fear that I harbored—one that had shattered the relationship with my brother two years earlier.

"So will you give it a try?" Kayla asked me at the end of our walk. "Before you leave, will you try Fortress and see what it's like yourself?

Surely there's a question you'd like to ask it, one that has nagged at you for a bit?"

I laughed nervously. "It's a bit like the Oracle at Delphi, isn't it?"

"Yes, except this oracle happens to know what it's talking about," Kayla said. "Fortress may not be able to predict the future, but it certainly has an educated opinion about it."

# CHAPTER TWENTY-EIGHT

Jude's sudden resignation as chairman of the Federal Reserve had shocked the world. The New York Stock Exchange stumbled badly after the announcement. Traders incorrectly assumed there was some type of institutional trouble ahead for the central banking system and reacted badly to the news. Blue-chip stocks lost nearly 10 percent of their value across the board.

It never occurred to them that Jude was simply bored with the job and ready for his next challenge.

When Jude resumed control of our company, he did so with a vengeance. In fact, he came back with such force, I decided to do something that had been unthinkable to me until then. I resigned from the board of Asher Enterprises. I took my private shares of stock with me, put them off to the side, and promptly forgot about them or what they were even worth.

Jude took my declaration of independence in stride. But the truth was that he didn't need me. He now had Singen and Isis advising him, along with a whole slew of additional regents of all shades and stripes. I'd been deadweight for years, I'd told him. There was no earthly reason I needed to remain a part of Asher Enterprises. He and I both knew that the driving force and engine was Jude—not me.

"You don't need me," I told him once I'd made my decision.

"True," he said. "But I like having you around. You know my secrets."

"I do. But so do others now."

Which was true. There was Singen, of course, and the other regents—although they didn't exactly count, because they were somewhat responsible for most of Jude's darkest secrets.

But Isis had become a near-constant companion to Jude since the state dinner at the White House. They were inseparable. Isis had become his closest advisor, closer even than Singen or any of the regents. And I assumed that she'd heard about, or knew, some of what I knew about Jude's life and ways.

I'd never asked Isis, of course. But I found it difficult to imagine that she could spend as much time as she did with Jude and not see how he conducted his affairs.

As I got to know Isis, my fascination with her only grew. She was—as much as any human being could be—a flawless individual. She never raised her voice in anger in any situation. Waiters and limo drivers adored her. Heads of state fawned over her. She never misspoke, either in private or public. I never heard her speak ill of a soul.

She was always dressed in the latest fashions, so much so that the paparazzi had begun to stake out her locations—as she shopped at stores on the Upper West Side or simply took in a new Broadway show—in order to send pictures to fashion magazines.

She was also as quick a study as anyone I'd ever met. Within months of meeting Jude, she'd essentially become a combination chief of staff, campaign manager, and public-relations director to him. Even from afar, I could tell she was stage-managing and directing every facet of Jude's professional and personal life.

She seemed too good to be true.

It was right about then that a slightly irrational and unlikely thought lodged itself within me—one that I simply could not remove, no matter how hard I tried.

I didn't dare confront Isis about it, but it became more apparent to me in every encounter and with every new interaction. In fact, over time, I'd come to the conclusion that there was no other explanation.

I thought about raising the question with Jude, but swiftly realized how foolish that would sound. It would likely end badly for me. I also didn't dare ask the question of Singen or any of the regents—not if they were in on the master plan. So I kept my mouth shut and merely watched their relationship evolve.

While it was more difficult for me to do now that I'd actively removed myself from the daily affairs of Asher Enterprises, I nevertheless could tell precisely what Jude was attempting. It became apparent to others who paid attention to such things as well.

Jude meant to become the richest man in the world.

As he'd been his entire life, he was patient at first and systematic. He began by leveraging Asher Enterprises holdings to purchase key companies that exploited every known natural resource on the planet. He took some of them privately, while he took other holdings of public companies he had no hope of actually controlling.

But in each case, the companies Jude selected quickly became industry leaders. The market responded. If Jude moved in on a company, it meant that it would soon establish itself as its industry's leader and others piled into the action.

Within a year or so after his resignation from the Fed, Jude either controlled or owned outright the leading oil, coal, and natural-gas companies. That industry, alone, moved him up to number eight on the *Forbes* list of the wealthiest billionaires in the world. But Jude wasn't done.

In short order, he consolidated three smaller companies to create the largest telecommunications company in the northern hemisphere. He then rolled up four computer companies to take over that dying industry and retooled the new company in order to directly challenge Apple's dominance in tablets, mobile devices, and laptops.

Those acquisitions moved him up to number four. But Jude still wasn't done. He had a plan, and his sights were set on the prize at the top. So he acquired two dying Internet giants that had failed to match Google and Facebook's pace of innovation, shook out all the cobwebs, and then turned them loose again on the darlings of Silicon Valley.

This put him over the top. Three years after he'd resigned as chairman of the Federal Reserve, and before our fortieth birthdays, Jude rose to number one on the *Forbes* list. He had the most toys, and he wasn't dead yet—not by any means.

But Jude still had one more small surprise in store for me, one that I'd been dreading. It would prove to separate us for good.

# CHAPTER TWENTY-NINE

"So what would you ask of Fortress, our modern-day Oracle of Delphi?" Kayla asked me playfully.

Her husband and Dr. Simons were there in the parallel-processing room to gauge my reaction to the power of the system that the programming community had built.

I couldn't help it. I was nervous. "How about the meaning of life?"

"Your life, or someone else's life?" asked Dr. Simons.

"I guess ours, in general," I offered lamely.

"Well, that's just silly," Kayla said bluntly, one hand on her hip. "And it's also not relevant. But give it a shot. See what Fortress does with it."

After some back and forth, Fortress determined what I'd really meant to genuinely ask about—namely, the much more humanistic question about the meaning of *my* life.

Fortress, at least, was able to determine that I didn't seem to care all that much about the general meaning of life—what it all meant; whether there were many gods or just one God; whether perfect good and evil even existed; the nature of the mind; or whether we had souls. In fact, Fortress fairly swiftly determined, for me, that what I really wanted to know was my own reason for even existing.

"Told you," Kayla said, one finger wagging at me. "So try something else."

"Yeah, that wasn't very satisfactory," Dr. Simons added. "Try something unexpected, something that only you would care about. That type of thing is what Fortress does best."

"Like what?" I asked.

"Like something that is important to you—and to no one else."

In our childhood, Jude and I had once watched an old film together. It proved to be one of Jude's favorites, perhaps of all time. It was a Hollywood epic with Richard Burton and Elizabeth Taylor about the lives of Marc Antony and Cleopatra. The film had been loosely based on Shakespeare's largely fictionalized account of Antony and Cleopatra.

But I'd wondered since seeing that film why it had captured Jude's heart. What was it about the film that struck such a deep chord within Jude? Was it the dangerous love affair between the queen of Egypt and a general vying to be an emperor god of the Roman Empire?

He and I had ended up talking about the film deep into the night. Jude had clearly been taken by the concept of exotic queens like Cleopatra and the notion of emperors who ruled as gods. "Why had they vanished from the earth?" Jude had wondered. "The Roman Empire was the last empire to rule all of the known, civilized world. There would almost certainly never be another. But why?" Jude had asked repeatedly.

In one fashion, we both concluded, it was actually the life of Jesus Christ—and the rise of Christianity to the point that it became the official religion of the Roman Empire—that had changed history and moved the civilized world in a vastly different direction. The life of one man had ended the world's last great empire. Christianity and the notion of one God replaced the pantheon of emperor gods in the Roman Empire, a movement that Constantine eventually codified in the third century. A later successor to Constantine's throne, Theodosius, was the last Roman emperor to rule all of known civilization.

"What makes a god?" I asked Dr. Simons.

"Do you mean a human being who is immortal?" he said. "Whose DNA code somehow lives forever?"

"Yes, in a fashion," I answered. "I know that you believe it will only be a matter of time before the human species is capable of cloning itself artificially. That I could, if I choose, become a creator of human life as I see fit. I could actually recreate myself—or anyone or anything else, for that matter. You, yourself, are probably capable of it today, right?"

"Yes, I am fully capable of it today—if I should choose to do so," Dr. Simons answered softly. "But I choose *not* to do so, though I daresay that there are others who will not make that same choice."

"So what is human life, then?" I asked. "And if we can create it so easily, in whatever fashion we choose and without any constraints, then have we become gods?"

Dr. Simons smiled and gestured toward the parallel processors. "Ask Fortress. See what it has to say about it. That's certainly a line of questioning I've never considered before, and I doubt anyone else has, either."

But I had a different, related question I wanted to ask—one I'd long suspected and which had separated me from Jude two years earlier.

"Who is Isis Kent?" I asked Fortress.

The answer, I learned, did not surprise me. It was the answer I'd guessed at two years earlier. It was the only thing that made any sense.

According to my eventual answer from Fortress, Isis Kent had never existed on earth in the way we thought of human existence—not until she'd become Jude's consort.

# Chapter Thirty

"I want you to be the best man at my wedding," Jude had said to me two years earlier, shortly after he'd achieved everything he'd set out to accomplish financially. "No one knows me like you. No one."

It had been less a request and more of a demand. But Jude had always been like that. He always got what he wanted. Nothing exceeded his grasp.

I'd known it was happening. It made all the sense in the world. It was logical. It made for a perfect union. Isis was clearly his companion, in every sense of the word.

Yet I wanted nothing to do with it. I couldn't quite explain it, even to myself. I had, quite literally, reached the very end of my ability to either care or deal with the realities of what I faced. I wanted out—and didn't know how.

When I looked at Jude, I saw a perfect, physical reflection of myself. He was more confident than me and generally more in command of his environment. But we were still the same—physically.

We were not, however, the same in the depth of our being. At least I'd hoped so, though I'd been unable to admit it until now. I'd largely been an observer, even of my own life, for a very long time. I'd been willing to stand by and watch Jude as he set out on first one path and then another—without any thought for what it might mean for me.

I was done. It was long past time for me to get a life of my own. And I had to start right now, here, in the presence of both Jude and the thing that, I knew, would control my brother's life for the remainder of his days.

Jude and Isis had invited me to their summer estate south of the nation's capital along the Potomac River to plan the wedding. The estate was near Mount Vernon, George Washington's summer home that was managed by a private nonprofit. Most of Washington's land had been preserved inside Mount Vernon, but not all. Jude and Isis had bought land nearby and had donated funds to restore parts of Washington's historic estate. Jude thought it fitting and somewhat amusing that he'd bought estate property once owned by the father of our country. He'd planted two rows of cherry trees on either side of the long driveway that led to the stately white manor house he'd built on the property.

When I'd arrived, a copy of *Forbes* magazine's annual list of the world's wealthiest people was tossed casually on the table in the entranceway. Jude's smiling, beatific face graced the cover.

"He made it," Isis said as she greeted me, took my hand expertly, pulled me close, and gave me an affectionate kiss on the cheek. Even with no one around to witness her beauty, she was still breathtaking. "Now we can turn our attention to the Good Earth campaign."

I had almost asked her—there in the hallway. But I didn't have the courage. I looked at her, felt the pull from her dark, deep eyes that had mesmerized me from the first moment I'd ever met her, and then averted my gaze. It was hopeless really. What could I possibly ask that would elicit a truthful answer?

Jude had already opened an expensive bottle of wine from the cellar to celebrate. He offered me a glass as I joined the two of them on the veranda.

They were well into their wedding planning by the time I'd arrived. It would be a wedding like no other, they'd decided.

"We've already heard from nearly one hundred world leaders," Isis said proudly. "They've all said yes. They'll all be there for the wedding."

"I don't think we've had a single person decline, right?" Jude added.

"Not yet," Isis said. "I can't imagine someone turning us down. We fully expect that most of the world's leaders will show up for it."

They were planning to be married at the high altar in Westminster Abbey. I wondered how that might even be possible—given that they weren't members of the Royal Family in the United Kingdom.

"Oh, we've gotten special dispensation from the queen," Isis said. "And I am, somewhat legitimately, part of the family. A distant part, but still. I was adopted into the House of Windsor. That should count for something."

"And if that doesn't work, I'll just join the Order of the Bath and become an honorary Knight of the Grand Cross. It isn't like knighthoods are all that difficult to come by anymore, not if they gave one to President Bush once," Jude said, laughing. "Of course, you *do* have to be pure in order to be bathed and enter in the knighthood. That could be a bit of a problem."

"Why there, at Westminster Abbey, of all places?" I asked them. "It seems a long way to go for a wedding."

"Well, it's halfway between New Zealand and America," Isis explained. "So why not? It will certainly be easier for the various world leaders traveling there from around the world."

"And everything is just a plane ride away, remember?" Jude had said to me with a wink. "Or have you forgotten?"

No, I hadn't forgotten. It was part of what was troubling me.

When Jude finally did ask whether I'd be his best man at their wedding, we were still out on the veranda—sitting in refurbished chairs that had once been part of the original White House centuries ago.

Lights from the nation's capital were somewhere off in the distance. It was peaceful and quiet. It reminded me of my first memories as a child, before the world had gotten so complicated and obscure.

"Do you remember that day, once, when we were kids on the farm in Waterford?" I asked him. "Do you remember that creature, the one that flew toward us and landed on the fence post near the house? I'd mentioned that it was such an ugly bird …"

"But it wasn't a bird," Jude answered. "Yes, of course. I remember."

I kept my gaze steady on Jude. I was afraid that if I looked in her direction, I wouldn't be able to go through with it. "Does she know about *them*?" I asked Jude. "Have you told her? Does she understand where your power and knowledge come from? Why you've been able to control the world as you have?"

"Do you mean Isis?" he said, throwing a glance her way before looking back at me.

"Yes. Does she know?"

Jude looked at me for a very long time. None of us spoke. I wasn't sure if it was because the question had surprised him or because he didn't know how to answer it.

"How could she *not* know, Thomas?" he finally said. "How is it possible that she could be my full and complete partner without that knowledge?"

"Does that matter to you, Thomas?" Isis asked me. "That I know? Is that what you are truly asking? Or is it something else entirely that you are trying to ask him—and me?"

I finally looked at Isis then, and I knew. In my heart, I knew. I also believed that my brother knew as well—but may not have cared.

"I can't be your best man," I told him. I stood. "I really and truly am sorry. I've been silent and complicit for far too long, and I can't be any longer. This isn't right, Jude. And I believe you've always known it."

I turned and left their home. I did not believe that I would ever return.

# CHAPTER THIRTY-ONE

Jude won his Senate race by the single biggest margin in the history of federal elections in New York. He was about to become the most famous freshman senator in Washington—ever.

I didn't call Jude to congratulate him. There was no need.

He wasn't even in office yet and the political analysts were already looking forward in time, wondering when he would run for president and the White House.

It was inevitable, they said. He had everything any national candidate could conceivably want—wealth, power, charisma, connections, a résumé without blemish, and a track record that appealed to every sector of the American electorate. He had a wife at his side whose star burned every bit as brightly.

Jude Asher was almost the perfect candidate for national office in America right now, at a time when politics at the national level seemed utterly broken. Every single post-election poll said precisely the same thing about him. The people trusted him. They believed his words. They seemed to relate to what he stood for, his values.

They expected Jude to save them financially. They expected him to lead them out of the wilderness of uncertainty, fear, and doubt. They expected him to rule with a strong and steady hand. And he would.

Jude won a plurality in nearly every conceivable demographic. Even Republicans generally liked him—mostly, it seemed, because he was like them. And Democrats adored him as well, because he seemed to care about them.

I would have paid close attention to all of this once. I would have wondered about it, thought about it, pulled it apart intellectually, and tried to sort through what it all really meant. But I didn't. Not now.

In another era and time, Jude would have made for a perfect emperor god. He'd mastered the banking, financial, economic, and business worlds. All that was left, really, was the political realm, and that would fall in relatively short order, I knew.

But the days of emperor gods had passed. Now someone like Jude needed to find other ways to amuse himself and control nation-states on a global basis. The game had changed in the past couple thousand years for the principalities and powers who wanted to rule the modern world.

# Chapter Thirty-Two

I made three phone calls while I waited for my flight out of the American Redoubt. I had one more trip to take before heading home to New York.

The first call was to John Hargrove, my editor.

"Did you find what you were looking for?" he asked me. "And more important, have you written it up? Am I going to see anything in print here at the paper?"

That was a good question. I hadn't yet made up my mind. It depended on whether I thought anyone would actually believe what I had to say.

"I have one more interview left," I answered. "I'll let you know when I'm done with it."

"But what did you find on your sabbatical? You were gone a while. You dropped off the grid. We wondered where you'd gone."

"Off the grid." I laughed. "Now that's funny."

"Yeah? Why?"

"It'll be in the story I file," I answered.

"So you are going to file something about what you found?"

"Maybe. Probably. We'll see," I said.

I could almost hear the questions that he really wanted to ask. But like everyone, he didn't want to pry into my personal life.

"So are you coming back to work at the newspaper?" he asked me finally. "I know you don't need the work. Good heavens, you can buy the paper with your spare change, most likely. But you're a good writer, Thomas. And we miss your perspective around here. It's … Well, it's different than what we would see otherwise."

That was an understatement. "Yeah, I'll be back, John. It's not like I have anything better to do. Might as well make you miserable."

My second call was to Frank Gore.

"So why didn't you just tell me about Fortress?" I asked him. "Why did you let me think the worst of a place like that?"

"Would you have believed me?" he asked. "You were so certain of what you'd find there. I figured it was easier for you to see it for yourself."

"Thanks," I said. "I appreciate it. Really. It renewed my faith in the basic goodness of humanity. I didn't think that was even possible. And I especially didn't think it would be possible there, in a part of the country that seems hell-bent on hiding from the world's troubles. It's nice to know that a place like that even exists—an open-source community."

"My pleasure," Frank said. "So what have you decided to write about? Do you know yet?"

I exhaled. "My editor just asked me that. Honestly, I don't know. Maybe just a piece of fiction, pretending to reveal truth. I guess it depends on how gullible people are and whether they prefer conspiracy theories over actual truth."

"Did you find the answers you were looking for on the Christian Brigades?" he asked. "I know that was frustrating you—what they're all about and how they figured into that attempt on your brother's life at the start of his political campaign."

"You know, I didn't—not really," I told him. "But I have one more interview left, and we'll see how far that takes me."

My third call was to Sandy.

"I miss you. I'm coming home," I said, glad to hear her voice.

"And will you be here for a while?" she asked. "Have you wandered around the country enough? Is it all out of your system now?"

"For the time being." I chuckled. "Next time, you're coming with me. I promise. There's a pretty spectacular place I want to show you. It's on the side of a mountain in Montana."

"Hmm," she said. "Sounds a bit dodgy."

"It isn't. It's anything but. You'll like it. Trust me. It isn't what you'd expect."

"If it's a place you like," she said, "that's enough for me. Sign me up. I'm happy to follow you to the ends of the earth, if that's what it takes to keep up with you."

"No need for that," I said, laughing. "But you'll like this place. It's extraordinary. Magical."

"Well, good," Sandy said. "I vote for magical any day."

# CHAPTER THIRTY-THREE

I was surprised that he'd even agreed to see me. I was even more surprised that he seemed lucid when I arrived at the small, windowless room at the far corner of the federal penitentiary reserved for high-profile prisoners in Reno, Nevada.

Samuel Chambers wasn't a typical prisoner, the warden told me beforehand. Most of the prisoners at their facility hadn't made it out of high school. Chambers, he told me, had a master's degree in religious philosophy from a good university and had already informed the prison's distance-learning staff that he intended to get his doctorate in divinity while he was incarcerated.

Chambers may have been crazy, but he wasn't stupid.

I'd read the transcripts of the FBI interviews with Chambers before I arrived at the prison for my own interview. There wasn't much there. He'd been silent and defiant, mostly, throughout those interviews.

Chambers had said next to nothing about either the Christian Brigades or why he'd tried to assassinate Jude that day in Battery Park. He also hadn't expressed any remorse whatsoever for the shooting.

I wasn't terribly hopeful that I'd find out anything useful during the course of my interview with him. But I had to at least try. I owed at least that to Jude, if nothing else. It was one final debt I felt compelled to pay.

Chambers was sitting patiently on a bench at a plain, gray table, his hands shackled and folded in front of him. His orange jumpsuit hung loosely around his thin frame. His eyes followed my movements closely as we came into the room.

The prison guard who escorted me told me to knock when I was ready to leave. I thanked him as he left and closed the door behind him. I looked at Chambers and glanced down at the floor. His ankles were shackled as well. They weren't taking any chances with this prisoner.

"Mr. Chambers, I wanted to thank you for taking the time today to visit with me," I began. I took a seat across the table. I pulled out my notebook, opened it, and then uncapped my pen and placed it beside me on the table. I turned on my digital recorder.

"My pleasure," he said. "I didn't have anything better to do today."

I smiled at him. Chambers didn't smile back. He just glared at me, sizing me up. I could tell he didn't know what to make of this visit yet.

"So I'm curious," I said. "I read your FBI interviews. You didn't say much during them."

"They weren't especially good questions," he said.

"You mean the questions were poor? Or they were the wrong ones?"

"Both. They just kept asking me why I'd done it, over and over. They made assumptions about both my motivations and my actions. And they were the wrong assumptions. So they kept getting the wrong answers."

"I see," I said thoughtfully. "I guess we're all a bit guilty of that at some point in our lives. For instance, I made some assumptions about the Christian Brigades before I went out West to look into it a bit. And what I found surprised me."

"I'll bet," Chamber snorted. "Especially when you consider that the Christian Brigades can't actually be found in a physical place."

"Not in a physical place?"

"You can't go find them somewhere, no more than anyone has ever been able to find the Knights Templar," Chambers said angrily.

I leaned forward. "But you're wrong, Samuel," I said carefully. "People *did* find the Knights Templar. They were in Jerusalem for years. They fought in the Crusades. They built things, ran banks. Many of them were burned at the stake for heresy before the pope disbanded their order. They were flesh and blood. And both church and state knew precisely who they were and where to find them."

Chambers took a deep breath. I thought, for a moment, that he would simply stop talking. He blinked furiously several times.

"I'm talking about now. Today," he said finally. "It's why the Christian Brigades exist on the earth. We exist in order to right the wrongs by any means necessary. We are the protectors. This is what we are meant to do."

*Now we're getting somewhere, even if it's based on conspiracy theories,* I thought. "So you think the Knights Templar order still exists today?" I asked. "You believe there are secret societies that control the world in some mysterious way? The Illuminati, Freemasons, the Bilderberg Group ... secret orders and societies that rule the planet?"

Chambers laughed. It came out more like a guttural croak. "You know," he said, "you, of all people, should watch what you say. If anyone knows the truth, it's you. They've had their eye on you for some time. They know all about you." He sat back then and just stared at me. I wasn't quite sure what he meant.

"I see," I said. "So you know about me. But what about Jude? How long have you had your eye on him? When did you, or the Christian Brigades, decide to assassinate my brother? When did you make that decision?"

This time, it was Chambers who leaned forward. His eyes glowed with an intensity that I hadn't seen until this very moment.

"See," he said with a fierceness that startled me, "that's *just* what I'm talking about. Of course they know all about Jude. They've known for a very long time. But what you're asking is precisely the wrong question. And if you keep asking it, you'll keep getting the wrong answer."

I did my best to stare down the palpable, unrestrained hatred welling up just a few feet from me. "So, Mr. Chambers, if I'm asking the wrong question, perhaps you can enlighten me. Help me out, please. What is the right question?"

Chambers smiled for the first time in our interview. This, too, surprised me. "You might start by asking me whom I was there to stop that day in Battery Park," he said. "You might ask me whom they told me I had to remove, because he was the only real threat standing in the way of what needs to be accomplished to bring order back into the world."

A slight chill settled in the room. "And who would that be?" I asked, fearful of the answer. "Who were you trying to kill that day in Battery Park, Mr. Chambers?"

"Why, it's you, of course," he said calmly. "I was there to stop *you*. That's what *they* told me to do. You're the one person anywhere on earth who could get in the way, who could keep him from doing what needs to be done and restore order. Because you know the truth. No one else is capable of stopping him. Only you."

I looked at Samuel Chambers sitting calmly across the table. I put my pen down and closed my notebook. I reached over and turned off the recorder.

I had my answer. It wasn't what I'd hoped for or even expected. But I had my answer. And, for now, that was enough.